RANDALLS ROUND

Eleanor Scott

OLEANDER PRESS

Oleander Press
16 Orchard Street
Cambridge
CB1 1JT

www.oleanderpress.com

First published in 1929
This edition published by Oleander Press, Cambridge, 2010
© Adam Leys. 2010. All Rights reserved.

ISBN: 9780900891953

Designed and typeset by Ayshea Carter
manganese@ntlworld.com

RANDALLS ROUND

Eleanor Scott

With an afterword by
Richard Dalby

CONTENTS

FOREWORD

THOUGH written at different times and under all sorts of conditions, these stories have all had their origin in dreams. They have, of course, been given shape, so that each forms a connected whole rather than a series of detached incidents or scenes: I do not know whether, by this adjustment, they have lost some of the horror experienced by the dreamer. But to give them shape was necessary; in dreams there is a kind of connecting thread so frail that no art can ever reproduce it - it is not possible to put it into the language and associations of waking life; and only in the first awakening, when one is, as it were, in the borderland between the world of dreams and the world of every day, remote from both yet understanding both as one never does when fully awake or fully asleep, can one remember the thread and try, however vainly, to translate it into terms of every day.

These dreams, as I say, were terrifying enough to the dreamer. I know what young Grindley endured in The Room because I myself have suffered that experience in a dream. I have sought for the clue of the Twelve Apostles; I have heard what Annis Breck heard at Queen's Garth, and seen more than Foster or M. Vétier saw on the beach at Kerouac. It may be that simply because these things were so terrifying I have failed to convey the horror I felt. I do not know. But I hope that some readers at least will experience an agreeable shudder or two in the reading of them.

Eleanor Scott

RANDALLS ROUND

"OF COURSE, I don't pretend to be aesthetic and all that," said Heyling in that voice of half contemptuous indifference that often marks the rivalry between Science and Art, "but I must say that this folk-song and dance business strikes me as pretty complete rot. I dare say there may be some arguments in favour of it for exercise and that, but I'm dashed if I can see why a chap need leap about in fancy braces because he wants to train down his fat."

He lit a cigarette disdainfully.

"All revivals are a bit artificial, I expect," said Mortlake in his quiet, pleasant voice, "but it's not a question of exercise only in this case, you know. People who know say that it's the remains of a religious cult – sacrificial rites and that. There certainly are some very odd things done in out-of-the-way places."

"How d'you mean?" asked Heyling, unconvinced. "You can't really think that there's any kind of heathen cult still practised in this country?"

"Well," said Mortlake, "there's not much left now. More in Wales, I believe, and France, than here. But I believe that if we could find a place where people had never lost the cult, we might run into some queer things. There are a few places like that," he went on, "places where they're said to perform their own rite occasionally. I mean to look it up some time. By the way," he added, suddenly sitting upright, "didn't you say you were going to a village called Randalls for the weekend?"

"Yes – little place in the Cotswolds somewhere. Boney gave me an address."

"Going to work, or for an easy?"

"Not to work. Boney's afraid of my precious health. He thinks I'm overworking my delicate constitution."

"Well, if you've the chance, I wish you'd take a look at the records in the old Guildhall there and see if you can find any references to folk customs. Randalls is believed to be one of the places where there is a genuine survival. They have a game I think, or a dance, called Randalls Round. I'd very much like to know if there are any written records – anything definite. Not if you're bored you know, or don't want to. Just if you're at a loose end."

"Right, I will," said Heyling; and there the talk ended.

It is unusual for Oxford undergraduates to take a long weekend off in the Michaelmas term with the permission of the college authorities; but Heyling, from whom his tutor expected great things, had certainly been reading too hard. The weather that autumn was unusually close and clammy, even for Oxford; and Heyling was getting into such a state of nerves that he was delighted to take the chance of getting away from Oxford for the weekend.

The weather, as he cycled out along the Woodstock Road, was moist and warm; but as the miles slipped by and the ground rose, he became aware of the softness of the air, the pleasant lines of the bare, sloping fields, the quiet of the low, rolling clouds. Already he felt calmer, more at ease.

The lift of the ground became more definite, and the character of the country changed. It became more open, bleaker; it had something of the quality of moorland, and the little scattered stone houses had that air of being one with the earth that is the right of moorland houses.

Randalls was, as Heyling's tutor had told him, quite a small place, though it had once boasted a market. Round a little square space, grass-grown now, where once droves of patient cattle and flocks of shaggy Cotswold sheep had stood to be sold, were grouped houses, mostly of the seventeenth or early eighteenth century, made of the beautiful mellow stone of the Cotswolds; and Heyling noticed among these one building of exceptional beauty, earlier in date than the others, long and low, with a deep square porch and mullioned windows.

"That's the Guildhall Mortlake spoke of I expect," he said to himself as he made his way to the Flaming Hand Inn, where his quarters were booked. "Quite a good place to look up town records. Queer how that sort of vague rot gets hold of quite sensible men."

Heyling received a hearty welcome at the inn. Visitors were not very frequent at that time of year, for Randalls is rather far from the good hunting country. Even a chance weekender was something of an event. Heyling was given a quite exceptionally nice room (or rather, a pair of rooms – for two communicated with one another) on the ground floor. The front one, looking out on to the old square, was furnished as a sitting-room; the other gave onto the inn yard, a pleasant cobbled place surrounded by a moss-grown wall and barns with beautiful lichened roofs. Heyling began to feel quite cheerful and vigorous as he lit his pipe and prepared to spend a lazy evening.

As he was settling down in his chair with one of the inn's scanty supply of very dull novels, he was mildly surprised to hear children's voices chanting outside. He reflected that Guy Fawkes' Day was not due yet, and that in any case the tune they sang was not the formless huddle usually produced on that august occasion. This was a real melody – rather an odd, plaintive air, ending with an abrupt drop that pleased his ear. Little as he knew folk-lore, and much as he despised it, Heyling could not but recognise that this was a genuine folk air, and a very attractive one.

The children did not appear to be begging; their song finished, they simply went away; but Heyling was surprised when some minutes later he heard the same air played again, this time on a flute or flageolet. There came also the sound of many feet in the market square. It was evident that the whole population had turned out to see some sight. Mildly interested, Heyling rose and lounged across to the bay window of his room.

The tiny square was thronged with villagers, all gazing at an empty space left in the centre. At one end of this space stood a man playing on a long and curiously sweet pipe: he played the same haunting plaintive melody again and again. In the very centre stood a pole, as a maypole stands in some villages; but instead of garlands and ribbons, this pole had flung over it the shaggy hide of some creature like an ox. Heyling could just see the blunt heavy head with its short thick horns. Then, without a word or a signal, men came out from among the watchers and began a curious dance.

Heyling had seen folk-dancing done in Oxford, and he recognised some of the features of the dance; but it struck him as being a graver, more barbaric affair than the performances he had seen before. It was almost solemn.

As he watched, the dancers began a figure that he recognised. They took hands in a ring, facing outwards; then, with their hands lifted, they began to move slowly round, counter-clockwise. Memory stirred faintly, and two things came drifting into Heyling's mind: one, the sound of Mortlake's voice as the two men had stood watching a performance of the Headington Mummers – "That's the Back Ring. It's supposed to be symbolic of death – a survival of a time when a dead victim lay in the middle and the dancers turned away from him." The other memory was dimmer, for he could not remember who had told him that to move in a circle counter-clockwise was unlucky. It must have been a Scot, though, for he remembered the word "widdershins."

These faint stirrings of memory were snapped off by a sudden movement in the dance going on outside. Two new figures advanced – one a man, whose head was covered by a mask made in the rough likeness of a bull; the other shrouded from head to foot in a white sheet, so that even the sex was indistinguishable. Without a sound these two came into the space left in the centre of the dance. The bull-headed man placed the second figure with its back to the pole where hung the hide. The dancers moved more and more slowly. Evidently some crisis of the dance was coming.

Suddenly the bull-headed man jerked the pole so that the shaggy hide fell outspread on the shrouded figure standing before it. It gave a horrid impression – as if the creature hanging limp on the pole had suddenly come to life, and with one swift, terrible movement had engulfed and devoured the helpless victim standing passively before it.

Heyling felt quite shocked – startled, as if he ought to do something. He even threw the window open, as though he meant to spring out and stop the horrid rite. Then he drew back, laughing a little at his own folly. The dance had come to an end: the bull-headed man had lifted the hide from the shrouded figure and thrown it carelessly over his shoulder. The flute-player had stopped his melody, and the crowd was melting away.

"What a queer performance!" said Heyling to himself. "I see now what old Mortlake means. It does look like a survival of some sort. Where's that book of his?"

He rummaged in his rucksack and produced a book that Mortlake had lent him – one volume of a very famous book on folk-lore. There were many accounts of village games and "feasts", all traced in a sober and scholarly fashion to some barbaric, primitive rite. He was interested to see how often mention was made of animal masks, or of the hides or tails of animals being worn by performers in these odd revels. There was nothing fantastic or strained in these accounts – nothing of the romantic type that Heyling scornfully dubbed "aesthetic." They were as careful and well authenticated as the facts in a scientific treatise. Randalls was mentioned, and the dance described – rather scantily, Heyling thought, until, reading on, he found that the author acknowledged that he had not himself seen it, but was indebted to a friend for the account of it. But Heyling found something that interested him.

"The origin of this dance," he read, "is almost certainly sacrificial. Near Randalls is one of those 'banks' or mounds, surrounded by a thicket, which the villagers refuse to approach. These mounds are not uncommon in the Cotswolds, though few seem to be regarded with quite as much awe as Randalls Bank, which the country people avoid scrupulously. The bank is oval in shape, and is almost certainly formed by a long barrow of the Paleolithic age. This theory is borne out by the fact that at one time the curious Randalls Round was danced about the mound, the 'victim' being led into the fringe of the thicket that surrounds it." (A footnote added, "Whether this is still the case I cannot be certain.") "Permission to open the tumulus has always been most firmly refused."

"That's amusing," thought Heyling, as he laid down the book and felt for a match. "Jove, what a lark it would be to get into that barrow!" he went on, drawing at his pipe. "Wonder if I could get leave? The villagers seem to have changed their ways a bit – they do their show in the village now. They mayn't be so set on their blessed mound as they used to be. Where exactly is the place?"

He drew out an ordnance map, and soon found it – a field about a mile and a half north-west of the village, with the word "Tumulus" in Gothic characters.

"I'll have a look at that tomorrow," Heyling told himself, folding up the map. "I must find out who owns the field, and get leave to investigate a bit. The landlord would know who the owner is, I expect."

Unfortunately for Heyling's plans, the next day dawned wet, although occasional gleams gave hope that the weather would clear later. His interest had not faded during the night, and he determined that as soon as the weather was a little better he would cycle out to Randalls Bank and have a look at it. Meanwhile, it might not be a bad plan to see whether the Guildhall held any records that might throw a light on his search as Mortlake had suggested. He accordingly hunted out a worthy who was, among many other offices, Town Clerk, and was led by him to the fifteenth century building he had noticed on his way to the Flaming Hand.

It was very cool and dark inside the old Guildhall. The atmosphere of the place pleased Heyling; he liked the simple groining of the roof and the worn stone stair that led up to the Record Room. This was a low, pleasant place, with deep windows and a singularly beautiful ceiling; Heyling noticed that it also served the purpose of a small reference library.

While the Town Clerk pottered with keys in the locks of chests and presses, Heyling idly examined the titles of the books ranged decorously on the shelves about the room. His eye was caught by the title, "Prehistoric Remains in the Cotswolds." He took the volume down. There was an opening chapter dealing with prehistoric remains in general, and, glancing through it, he saw mentions of long and round barrows. He kept the book in his hand for closer inspection. He really knew precious little about barrows, and it would be just as well to find out a little before beginning his exploration. In fact, when the Town Clerk left him alone in the Record Room, that book was the first thing he studied.

It was a mere text-book, after all, but to Heyling's ignorance it revealed a few facts of interest. Long barrows, he gathered, were older than round, and more uncommon, and were often objects of superstitious awe among the country folk of the district, who generally opposed any effort to explore them; but the whole chapter was very brief and skimpy, and Heyling had soon exhausted its interest.

The town records, however, were more amusing, for he very soon found references to his particular field. There was a lawsuit in the early seventeenth century which concerned it, and the interest to Heyling was redoubled by the vagueness of certain evidence. A certain Beale brought charges of witchcraft against "diuers Persouns of y^s Towne." He had reason for alarm, for apparently his son, "a yong and comely Lad of 20ann.", had completely disappeared: "wherefore ye sd. Jno. Beale didd openlie declare and state y^t ye sd. Son Frauncis hadd been led away by Warlockes in ye Daunce (for y^t his Ringe, ye wh. he hadd long worne, was found in ye Fielde wh. ye wot of) and hadd by y^m beene done to Deathe in y^r Abhominable Practicinges." The case seemed to have been hushed up, although several people cited by "ye sd. Jno. Beale" admitted having been in the company of the missing youth on the night of his disappearance – which, Heyling was interested to notice, was that very day, 31st October.

Another document, of a later date, recorded the attempted sale of the "field wh. ye wot of" – (no name was ever given to the place) – and the refusal of the purchaser to fulfil his contract owing to "ye ill repute of the place, the wh. was unknowen to Himm when he didd entre into his Bargayn."

The only other documents of interest to Heyling were some of the seventeenth century, wherein the authorities of the

Commonwealth inveighed against "ye Lewd Games and Dauncyng, ye wh. are Seruice to Sathanas and a moste strong Abhominatioun to ye Lorde." These spoke openly of devil worship and "loathlie Ceremonie at ye Banke in ye Fielde." It seemed that more than one person had stood trial for conducting these ceremonies, and against one case (dated 7th November, 1659) was written, "*Conuicti et combusti.*"

"Good Lord – burnt!" exclaimed Heyling aloud. "What an appalling business! I suppose the poor beggars were only doing much the same thing as those chaps I saw yesterday."

He sat lost in thought for some time. He thought how that odd tune and dance had gone on in this remote village for centuries; had there been more to it once, he wondered? Did that queer business with the hide mean – well, some real devilry? Pictures floated into his mind – odd, squat little men, broad of shoulder and long of arm, naked and hairy, dancing in solemn, ghastly worship, dim ages ago... This business was getting a stronger hold of him than he would have thought possible.

"Strikes me that if there is anything of the old devilry left, it'll be in that field," he concluded at last. "The dance they do now is all open and above board; but if they still avoid the field, as that book of Mortlake's seems to think, that might be a clue. I'll find out."

He rose and went down to inform the Town Clerk that his researches were over, and then went back to the inn in a comfortable frame of mind. Certainly his weekend was bringing him distraction from his work: no thought of it had entered his head since he first heard the children singing outside the inn.

The landlord of the Flaming Hand was a solid man who gave the impression of honesty and sense. Heyling felt that he could depend upon him for a reasonable account of "the fielde which ye wot of." He accordingly tackled him after lunch, and was at once amused, surprised and annoyed to find that the man hedged as soon as he was questioned on the subject. He quite definitely opposed any idea of exploration.

"I'm not like some on 'em, sir," he said. "I wouldn't go for to say that it'd do any 'arm for you to take a turn in the field while it was light, like. But it ain't 'ealthy after dark, sir, that field aren't. Nor it ain't no sense to go a-diggin' and a-delvin' in that there bank. I've lived in this 'ere place a matter of forty year, man and boy, and I know what I'm a-sayin' of."

"But why isn't it healthy? Is it marshy?"

"No, sir, it ain't not to say marshy."

"Don't the farmers ever cultivate it?"

"Well, sir, all I can say is I been in this place forty year, man and boy, and it ain't never been dug nor ploughed nor sown nor reaped in my mem'ry. Nor yet in my father's, nor in my grandfather's. Crops wouldn' do, sir, not in that field."

"Well, I want to go and examine the mound. Who's the owner? – I ought to get his leave, I suppose."

"You won't do that, sir."

"Why not?"

" 'Cause I'm the owner, sir, and I won't 'ave anyone, not the King 'isself nor yet the King's son, a-diggin' in that bank. Not for a waggon-load of gold, I won't."

Heyling saw it was useless.

"Oh, all right! If you feel like that about it!" he said carelessly.

The stubborn, half-frightened look left the host's eyes.

"Thank you, sir," he said, quite gratefully.

But he had not really gained the victory. Heyling was as obstinate as he, and he had determined that before he left Randalls he would have investigated that barrow. If he could not get permission, he would go without. He decided that as soon as darkness fell he would go out on the quiet and explore in earnest. He would borrow a spade from the open cart-shed of the inn – a spade and a pick, if he could find one. He began to feel some of the enthusiasm of the explorer.

He decided that he would spend part of the afternoon in examining the outside of the mound. It was not more than a ten minutes' ride to the field, which lay on the road. It was, as the landlord had said, uncultivated. Almost in the middle of it rose a mass of stunted trees and bushes – a thick mass of intertwining boughs that would certainly take some strength to penetrate. Was it really a tomb, Heyling wondered? And he thought with some awe of the strange prehistoric being who might lie there, his rude jewels and arms about him.

He returned to the inn, his interest keener than ever. He would most certainly get into that barrow as soon as it was dark enough to try. He felt restless now, as one always does when one is looking forward with some excitement to an event a few hours distant. He fidgeted about the room, one eye constantly on his watch.

He wanted to get to the field as soon as possible after dark, for his casual inspection of the afternoon had shown him that the task of pushing through the bushes, tangled and interwoven as they were, would be no light one; and then there was the opening of the tumulus to be done – that soil, untouched by spade or plough for centuries, to be broken by the pick until an entrance was forced into the chamber within. He ought to be off as soon as he could safely secure the tools he wanted to borrow.

But Fate was against him. There seemed to be a constant flow of visitors to the Flaming Hand that evening – not ordinary labourers dropping in for a drink, but private visitors to the landlord, who went through to his parlour behind the bar and left by the yard at the side of the inn. It really did seem like some silly mystery story, thought Heyling impatiently; the affair in the marketplace, the landlord's odd manner over the question of the field, and now this hushed coming and going from the landlord's room!

He went to his bedroom window and looked out into the yard. He wanted to make quite sure that the pick and spade were still in the open cart-shed. To his relief they were; but as he looked he got yet another shock. A man slipped out from the door of the inn kitchen and slipped across the yard into the lane that lay behind the inn. Another followed him, and a little later another; and all three had black faces. Their hands showed light, and their necks; but their faces were covered with soot, so that the features were quite indistinguishable.

"This is too mad!" exclaimed Heyling half aloud. "Jove, I didn't expect to run into this sort of farce when I came here. Wonder if *all* old Cross's mysterious visitors have had black faces? Anyway, I wish they'd buck up and clear out. I may not have another chance to go to that mound if I don't get off soon."

The queer happenings at the inn now appeared to him solely as obstacles to his own movements. If their import came into his mind at all, it was to make him wonder whether there were any play like a mummers' show which the village kept up; or games, perhaps, like those played in Scotland at Hallowe'en... By Jove! That probably was the explanation. It *was* All Hallows' Eve! Why couldn't they buck up and get on with it, anyhow?

His patience was not to be tried much longer. Soon after nine the noises ceased; but to make doubly sure, Heyling did not leave his room till ten had struck from Randalls church.

He got cautiously out of his bedroom window and landed softly on the cobbles of the yard. The tools still leaned against the wall of the open shed – trusting man, Mr. Cross, of the Flaming Hand! The shed where his cycle stood was locked, though, and he swore softly at the loss of time this would mean in getting to the field. It would take him twenty-five minutes to walk.

As a matter of fact, it did not take him quite so long, for impatience gave him speed. The country looked very beautiful under the slow-rising hunter's moon. The long bare lines of the fields swept up to the ridges, black against the dark serene blue of the night sky. The air was cool and clean, with the smell of frost in it. Heyling, hurrying along the rough white road, was dimly conscious of the purity and peace of the night.

At last the field came in sight, empty and still in the cold moonlight. Only the mound, black as a tomb, broke the flood of light. The gate was wide open, and even in his haste this struck Heyling as odd.

"I could have sworn I shut that gate," he said to himself. "I remember thinking I must, in case anyone spotted I'd been in. It just shows that people don't avoid the place as much as old Cross would like me to believe."

He decided to attack the barrow on the side away from the road, lest any belated labourer should pass by. He walked round the mound, looking for a thin spot in its defence of thorn and hazel bushes; but there was none. The scrub formed a thick belt all round the barrow, and was so high that he could not see the top of the mound at all. The confounded stuff might grow half-way up the tumulus for all he could see.

He abandoned any idea of finding an easy spot to begin operations. It was obviously just a question of breaking through. Then, just as he was about to take this heroic course, he stopped short, listening. It sounded to him as if some creature were moving within the bushes – something heavy and bulky, breaking the smaller branches of the undergrowth.

"Must be a fox, I suppose," he thought, "but he must be a monster. It sounds more like a cow, though of course it can't be. Well, here goes."

He turned his back to the belt of thick undergrowth, ducked his head forward, and was just about to force his backwards way through the bushes when again he stopped to listen. This time it was a very different sound that arrested him – it was the distant playing of a pipe. He recognised it – the plaintive melody of Randalls Round.

He paused, listening. Yes – feet were coming up the road – many feet, pattering unevenly. There *was* some village game afoot, then!

The words of Mortlake's book came back to his mind. The author had said that at one time the barrow was the centre of the dance. Was it possible that it was so still – that there was a second form, less decorous perhaps, which took place at night?

Anyhow, he mustn't be seen, that was certain. Lucky the mound was between him and the road. He stole cautiously towards the hedge on the far side of the field. Thank goodness it was a hedge and not one of those low stone walls that surround most fields in the Cotswolds.

As he took cautious cover he couldn't help feeling a very complete fool. Was it really necessary to take this precaution? And then he remembered the look of stubborn determination on the landlord's face. Yes, if he were to investigate the barrow he must keep dark. Besides, there might be something to see in this business – something to delight old Mortlake's heart.

The tune came nearer, and the sound of footsteps was muffled. They were in the grassy field, then. Heyling cautiously raised his head from the ditch where he lay; but the mound blocked his view as yet. What luck that he'd happened to go to Randalls just at that time – Hallowe'en! He remembered the documents in the Guildhall, and Jno. Beale's indictment of the men who, he averred, had made away with his son at Hallowe'en. Heyling's blood tingled with excitement.

The playing came closer, and now Heyling could see the figures of men moving into the circle they formed for Randalls Round. Again he was struck by the queer barbaric look of the thing and by the gravity of their movements; and then his heart gave a sudden heavy thump. The dancers had all the blackened mask-like faces of the men he had seen leaving the inn. How odd! thought Heyling. They perform quite openly in the village square, and then steal away at night, disguising their faces...

The dance was extraordinarily impressive, seen in that empty field under the quiet moon. There was no sound but the whispering of their feet on the long dry grass and the melancholy music of the pipe. Then, quite suddenly, Heyling heard again the cracking, rustling sound from the dense bushes about the mound. It was exactly like the stirring of some big clumsy animal. The dancers heard it too; there came a sort of shuddering gasp; Heyling saw one man glance at his neighbour, and his eyes shone light and terrified in his blackened face.

The melody came slower, and with a kind of horror Heyling knew that the crisis of the dance was near. Slowly the dancers formed the ring, their faces turned away from the mound; then from outside the circle came a shrouded figure led by a man wearing a mask like a bull's head. The veiled form was led into the ring. The pipe mourned on.

Again, shattering the quiet, came a snapping, crashing noise from the inmost recesses of the bushes about the barrow. There *was* some big animal in there, crashing his way out...

Then he saw it, bulky and black in the pure white light – some horrible primitive creature, with heavy lowered head. The dancers

21

circled slowly; the air of the flute grew faint.

Heyling felt cold and sick. This was loathsome, devilish... He buried his head in his arms and tried to drown the sound of that mourning melody.

Sounds came through the muffling hands over his ears – a crunching, tearing sound, and then a horrible noise like an animal lapping. Sweat broke out on Heyling's back. It sounded like bones... He could not think, or move, or pray... The haunting music still crooned on...

The crashing, snapping noise again as the branches broke. *It*, whatever it was, was going back into its lair. The tune grew fainter and fainter. Steps sounded again on the road – slow steps, with no life in them. The horrible rite was over.

Very cautiously Heyling got to his feet. His knees trembled, and his breath came short and rough. He felt sick with horror and with personal fear as he skirted the mound. His fascinated eyes saw the break in the hazels and thorns; then they fell upon a dark mark on the ground – dark and wet, soaking into the dry grass. A white rag, dappled with dark stains, lay near...

Heyling could bear no more. He gave a strangled cry as he rushed, blindly stumbling, falling sometimes, out of the field and down the road.

THE TWELVE APOSTLES

THE American visitor looked up from the specification book.

"That seems all square," he said; "genuine old English stuff. But there's one thing, sir, you haven't mentioned that I've just got to have."

He looked at the house agent with a paternal smile.

"Well, sir, I think I've told you all details," said Mr. Gibson. He would not entrust this wealthy client to the tender care of a mere clerk; he was too rare a find. "Still, I'm sure," he went on persuasively, "that Mr. Langtre, the owner of the Manor, would be glad to meet you in any reasonable alterations or repairs."

Mr. Matthews smiled a little and his nice eyes twinkled.

"I'm sure, from what you tell me, that's so," he replied. "Only I'm afraid he couldn't have anyone put in just the detail I'm thinking of. Mr. Gibson, I want a real good ghost."

Mr. Gibson looked distinctly less rubicund.

"A-a ghost?" he stammered, his eyes wandering.

"What? You don't mean to say there is one?" cried the shrewd client.

"Well, sir – with an old place like the Manor – genuine sixteenth century... What I mean to say is, there's always fools about in a country place..."

"But there is – well, a story? I warn you, sir, I shan't buy the place unless there is."

Poor Mr. Gibson fidgeted uneasily. Who could have foreseen

such a difficulty as this?

"Well, you see, sir, how it is," he said at last, "Mr. Langtre did give me most strict orders as nothing was to be said. Most strict. Still, sir, seeing what your conditions are, I don't mind saying that things – well, things are said about the Manor as had better not be said."

"That's a bit vague," said the American. "I don't want any doubts about this thing. I want a real good Old English slap-up ghost, and I don't mind paying a bit for it. Why, who'd give two rows of pins for an Elizabethan manor without a ghost in it?"

Mr. Gibson was understood to mutter something about "a matter of opinion." Then, taking his courage in both hands, he said desperately:

"I tell you what, sir. You come along with me to the Vicar. He's what they call an antiquarian, and he knows all about the Manor. You see, I'm bound not to tell anything; and truth to tell I don't know much. But Mr. Molyneux, he'll tell you everything there is to know about Sir Jerome's room."

The worthy house agent took his respectable bowler, and the two men went up the broad tree-lined main street of Much Barton, Gibson discoursing the while on the old-world atmosphere of the place. The American was certainly nibbling: it wouldn't be the agent's fault if Barton Cross Manor remained unsold.

The Vicar was in, and received his visitors in a book-lined study that might have come out of one of Trollope's novels: and Mr. Matthews, summing him up with a business man's acumen, came to his topic at once.

"Ghost at the Manor?" said Mr. Molyneux, fingering his chin. "Well, it wouldn't be surprising if there were. In fact, if one can rely on the evidence of an ignorant soldier and a jealous parish priest, there certainly were once some very – er – peculiar happenings in the priest's room."

Mr. Matthews preserved an intelligent silence, and the Vicar continued:

"The story goes that early in the reign of Elizabeth Mr. Everard Langtre, the then Squire of the Manor, had in his household a private chaplain, commonly called Sir Jerome, or Jeremy. 'Sir' was then, as you doubtless know, a courtesy title of Priests of the – er – Roman persuasion."

"Sir – I mean, Mr. – Everard Langtre was a Roman, then?" asked the American.

"He was," answered the Vicar, "and had, as was then customary, his private oratory and his private chaplain. Now this chaplain, Jeremy Lindall, seems to have been a man of very curious disposition. He was, like many another private chaplain of the time, a chemist of no little originality and skill. Stories about him were rife, of course – he does not seem to have been popular – and he was credited with witchcraft, demonology, traffic with the powers of evil, and so on. He certainly did go in for some very curious experiments, in which gold seems to have been a necessary ingredient: and it was said that he used in this way all his private stock of gold until at last he became so ragged that he had to keep within doors. This, one gathers, was no loss. His early – er – Mass over, he had the whole day free to conduct his chemical experiments or work his spells in the large chamber that was given up to him. The fact that he asked to be given a room facing north told against him greatly with the villagers."

"Why?" asked Mr. Matthews.

"Why, because it was considered the best aspect for devil-worship. Have you never noticed that in country churchyards there are no graves on the north side of the church? – Well, to continue. Sir Jerome seems to have gradually become quite a recluse; and when he died, which was in the year 1562, there was a curious scene at his burial. All sorts of things were said, as is always the case in these stories of chemists, misunderstood and maligned, their actions and words distorted through generations of rustic folk."

"Such as –?"

"Oh, that his dead face wore a look of terror and pain beyond human endurance: and the beldame who laid out the corpse for burial was so powerfully affected that she was stricken dumb, and died a few weeks later. No one could be persuaded to carry the body to the grave for some time, but at last four stout men were bribed into doing it. The story goes – But wait: I'll read it to you–"

He turned to a large desk and pulled out a drawer.

"This is an account of the burial written at the time by the parish priest of Much Barton," he said. "The original manuscript is in Mr. Langtre's possession: but I made the copy myself, and I will vouch for its accuracy."

He spread the sheets out before him.

"Of course," he interpolated, looking up with his *pince-nez* in his hand, "you will understand that the parish priest, a hard-working and humble person enough, was no doubt a little jealous of the gentleman of leisure up at the Manor. You must take his account *cum grano*. Well, then – the beginning is torn away, but the context is clear enough.

" ' ...did with utmoste payne perswayd foure stoute Carles to ye Worke, and soe didd enforce Kit Harcott, Hodge Payne with his bro. Willm. and Ned Greene to engage to carrye ye Coffre to ye Churche, where I hadde all Thinges needefull for ye Buriall. But when these came, lo they bore no Coffre, but they were alle sweatinge and Tremblinge in suche Fearfulle wise that I was faine to Conforte them, saying that verelie Sir Hiereme must be a Starke Mann and Stoute when his deade Bodie gar'd Stronge Carles soe to Shake and to Sweate. Whereat Kit, Tis not his Weyghte, goode father, quoth he, for a man to be heavie is no suche mattere. But ye Coffre is lighte as it were emptie; and in soothe we had almoste opend it, fearinge we shou'de be att oure paynes for no goode; but thatt (And here he soe Shooke that his voyce dy'd in his Throote.)

"'Come mann a Goddes mercie, quoth I to hearten him, there is noughte to Tremble att in thatt youre worke hath beene so lyghte. Ay but, (quoth he) there came a sounde in ye Boxe lyke to a litel whisperyng or rustelyng, soe thatt we didd put it downe in feare. And soe we kneel'd and sayd a Pater and an Aue: and Ned (who is an Acolyth and deuoute) wou'd saye the De Profundis: but when we sayd *Requiem aeternam dona ei Dñe* there came soe dreadfull a Laughe that we felle forwarde in great feare. But when after a space we didd lifte our selues, lo we sawe a slimie trayl as of an huge Slugge or Snayl coming out from ye Coffre.'

"The story goes on," said Mr. Molyneux, "with an account, of more interest to a cleric than a layman, of the burial rites. No doubt the slight mystery surrounding the life of the recluse, his chemical experiments, his retirement and so on, had pre-disposed the simple folk, both priest and people, to see signs and wonders: anyhow, the parish priest, Sir Edgar Knox, gives quite a lurid account of the burial service: how the holy water left a trail as of slime across the coffin: how the holy candles went out and a heavy smoke dragged across the church: and how the terrified boys serving at the altar saw in the thick greasy vapour dim shapes twisting about the coffin; and he says that in answer to each prayer he heard, instead of 'Amen,' a devilish laugh, 'highe and shrille like a Peeuishe Shrewe.' In fine, he could not take it on himself to bury Sir Jerome in the consecrated ground, where lay the bodies of the simple village folk; and so he laid the poor corpse in that dim and unhallowed region that lies north of the church, 'that he who had Choasen ye northe in his Lyfe myghte have it alsoe in his Deth.' And there he lies, I have no doubt, to this day."

Mr. Molyneux laid down the manuscript and took off his glasses. His face was flushed with the enthusiasm of the antiquarian.

"It's a good story," commented the American. "But it seems to me that Sir Jerome's ghost, if he has run to one, would walk in the 'dim and unhallowed region' – if I may use your words, sir – in the churchyard, rather than in the Manor."

"No doubt," answered the Vicar, "if that were all. But there is more to come.

"Later in Elizabeth's reign the Langtres came into bad odour in connection with the Throgmorton Plot. The Manor, like many another Roman Catholic mansion, was ransacked for evidence. Little enough was found in the house except the plate in the chapel; and even that proved not to be genuine gold and silver. But among the soldiers who searched the house was one Job Harcott, who was a descendant or connection of the Kit Harcott who had carried Sir Jerome's coffin. This man remembered the tales of the chaplain's chemical experiments: and it occurred to him, sacrilegious as it sounds, that the gold plate of the chapel might have been taken for some such experiment. So he secretly left the party of soldiers and went back alone to the Manor to search for the treasure, which he believed (for so the tradition went) to be hidden in the priest's own room.

"What exactly happened to Job Harcott no one will ever know. He was missed after dusk. A crony of his, one Ezra Minshull, then remembered a conversation he had had with the miserable man. He reports it thus:

"'This Minshull remember'd him that Harcott whyl he was yet with us had sayd that he was but litel astonied that ye Playt was contrefeyt: for (quoth he) when a Mann lusteth after Golde (as I haue herd this Hierime didd) he leaueth not his Luste, but hathe it euer in his Presence. Soe that when aftre longe seekyng we cou'd by noe means find Harcott, Minshull perswayding us, we return'd to ye Manour to see what shou'd be in Sir Hierime's room where he abode.'"

"Well?" interjected the American.

Mr. Molyneux looked up, arrested by the tone of his visitor.

"They found Harcott. His body was lying in the passage that leads from the priest's room: he seemed to have been running away from the room down the passage. He was quite dead."

There was a moment's silence, and then the Vicar continued:

"Sir, I am an old man. I have read many curious books and seen many curious things. I ask you with all the earnestness of which I am capable not to pry into this matter. Buy the house if you will – you will be doing a kindness to my old friend Godfrey Langtre and taking a step that you will not, I think, regret: but, as you value your life and your sanity, avoid that accursed room."

He paused, flushed with the embarrassment of a shy man who interferes in another's affairs.

"Sir, I'm grateful, real grateful, to you," said the American, "and I'll bear in mind what you've said. You've impressed me. But I'm interested, and I'll buy that house right now, lock, stock and barrel. And I hope, sir, that you'll do me the great kindness to come and see me sometimes. I won't trespass on your time any more now. Goodbye, sir, and thank you."

So Mr. Matthews became the owner of Barton Cross Manor.

If the house was not quite as attractive seen in the dusk of a drizzling October afternoon as it had appeared in the mellow sunshine of September, certainly Mr. Gibson could not be blamed for the fact. Nor could Mr. Langtre. Yet Mr. Matthews felt that he wanted to blame someone for the discomfort of the chill rooms with their stiff and unwelcoming air and suspicious atmosphere. Presently he put it down to the attitude of a couple, mother and son, who had been caretakers at the Manor, and who no doubt objected to having to do a little work, besides opening windows and airing rooms, in exchange for the wages the Langtre family allowed them. In fact, thought the American, sniffing the close air of the passages, they didn't seem really keen on doing even that.

He ordered a fire in the library and another in his bedroom, and, when these were well alight and snapping and blazing cheerily, he opened the windows wide and let in waves of cool rainy air, laden with faint scents of late roses and dying leaves and wet earth. The panelled walls shone in the warm firelight; the well-filled bookcases invited him. He began to feel really comfortable and at home, and went for a little psycho-analytic speculation on the subject of Atmosphere and its Influence on Human Sensation. Mr. Matthews was the type of man who likes such phrases, especially when written with capital letters. They made him feel profound.

This comfortable mood lasted him until ten the next morning, when, warm and contented after a "real English" breakfast followed by an indisputable cigar, he decided to spend the morning in a survey of the house.

The morning was dark, with a threatening sky; though the rain was not actually falling, it looked as though the lowering clouds were only allowing a respite to the garden battered by yesterday's downpour, and might stream again at any minute. It seemed a most suitable day to re-examine his property, which, like many Tudor manor-houses, needed much exploration before its plan was really known.

Mr. Matthews wandered about over the ground floor, very contentedly losing his way in passages and communicating rooms, until he knew it thoroughly. He then proceeded to the next.

This was easier, since it had suffered less from later incongruous additions. It was roughly in the shape of a cross, the arms of which were composed of four passages running north, south, east and west, and radiating from a square well which looked down to the hall below. The south passage was so short as hardly to be a passage at all, and the north corridor was correspondingly long. Mr. Matthews' own bedroom was at the junction of the north and west corridors, with a door leading into each; and by the door in the north passage there was a kind of small shrine – a large crucifix, a priedieu chair, some candles and flowers. The whole house, in fact, bore signs of the religion of its late owners: Mr. Matthews had never before seen so many holy water stoups, for instance. There was one outside every door, and even one on the wall opposite the shrine – a blank wall with no door in it.

Going along the north passage, Mr. Matthews soon discovered the reason for the absence of doors in the east wall. It was the wall of the old chapel, which ran the whole length of the corridor, and whose door was in the northern end of the east wall. It was dismantled now, and all the decorations gone; and the American thought he could still see traces of the scars left by the soldiers who had ransacked the chapel for the lost treasure. He stood at the door, picturing the scene to himself; and then, as the whole story filtered back into his mind, he realised that he must be standing near, if not on, the very spot where the returning band had found the body of Job Harcott.

That door, at the end of the passage, must lead into the priest's room. Mr. Matthews felt quite a thrill as he thought of the lonely chemist, labouring in that remote chamber at his terrible experiments, abandoned and feared by his neighbours, dying at last, desolate even in his death. Mr. Matthews was not an imaginative man; but somehow, standing there in the dim passage, the melancholy rain pattering faintly outside, he could enter into the mind of the long-dead priest, fanatical with his dreadful enthusiasms, his mad, soul-destroying experiments, renouncing all happiness in this world or a possible next in exchange for that power which it is unlawful to possess. And the modern American thought he could understand some of the ambition, the horror, the enthusiasm, the desolation and despair, which had made up that man's soul.

Closing the door of the chapel, he continued his investigations. The door at the end of the north passage was locked, and he made a mental note to ask Mrs. Sharpe, the caretaker, for the key. The other doors in the passage, that is those in the west wall, led to rooms whose close air and antique style of furnishing led him to the conclusion that they had not been used for many years; in fact the first room that gave signs of recent use was his own bedroom at the corner of the square well.

"That's queer," thought the American. "It's not as if that set of rooms faced north, for naturally they face west. I'd have understood it if the rooms in the west corridor, now, had been neglected; but they're quite fresh. Guess they're odd folk, these Langtres." And with that he dismissed the matter from his mind. He remembered, however, to ask for the missing key of the locked door; and, meeting Sharpe himself on the stairs, he mentioned it there and then.

Sharpe changed colour, apparently confused at having been discovered remiss in his duty, and insisted on accompanying the new tenant back to the north passage.

"This room ain't much used, sir, 'aving a north aspeck," he said apologetically as he turned the key. It squealed rustily in the lock, and Matthews, happening to glance at the man's face, was startled to see it white and wet with sweat.

"Why, man, what's wrong?" he cried.

The colour crept back to Sharpe's face.

"It's me 'eart, sir," he panted. "Any effort'll make me go all any'ow for a minute. But it goes off, sir, straight away. It don't last." He glanced anxiously in the direction of his employer. Mr. Matthews grunted and said no more.

The locked room was indeed in need of airing. A whiff of dank air with a curiously mouldy smell greeted them: so earthy a smell that the American looked instinctively at the walls for traces of damp.

"I suppose it's because of the damp that they don't use the room," he said with a glance around him.

It was very obviously unused. It had very little furniture, and what there was looked old. There was an oak chair, a heavy table, and a kind of desk or cabinet, with a cupboard rising from a flat tabletop. The walls, however, showed no signs of damp: the panels were not warped or cracked, nor were the rather odd carvings on them at all defaced.

"I believe, if it were regularly warmed and aired, it would be as good a room as any, and most interesting," declared the American. "Anyway, we'll try. It's a real unique room. Do as you did with the other rooms, Sharpe – light a real good fire and open the windows and door to get a through draught. I've regularly taken to this room," he went on as he examined the panelling more closely. "Shouldn't wonder if I move in here when you get it fixed right."

"The fam'ly don't consider it 'ealthy, sir, not this room," muttered Sharpe.

He had to clear his throat before he could make his voice sound at all; and Mr. Matthews, struck by the man's agitation, was suddenly seized by a suspicion. Why were the Sharpes so keen to keep him out of the room? Had they some motive for wishing to deny access to it to anyone but themselves?

"You do as I say," he said, not peremptorily, but quite firmly. "I don't take back my orders without a good reason," he added.

Halfway down the corridor, he heard the grating of the key in the rusty lock of the closed door.

"Here, Sharpe! I said that room was to be left open and aired," he said, turning sharply.

"Beg pardon, sir... I thought, seein' as it was wet, I'd best leave it shut till I got a fire goin', sir," muttered the servant.

"Well... But, hang it, man, why lock the door when it's so stiff? Go back and – No, never mind. Give me the key."

Taking it from the man's shaking hand, Mr. Matthews went back down the corridor, and, with some difficulty, opened the door.

"There," he said as he rejoined Sharpe. "Get a fire on in there when you've time, and leave it open all day. I bet we'll get rid of that rank smell..." He stopped short, startled by the extraordinary expression in Sharpe's eyes. "Why, Sharpe!" he began; but even as he spoke the man dropped his eyes and with an effort regained his composure.

"Very good, sir," he murmured; and the baffled American went back to the library.

The rain lifted in the afternoon, with a sky that gave promise of a fine morrow: and Mr. Matthews went out for a long walk to visit certain places of local interest. It was not until he had finished a cosy tea and a cigarette that it occurred to him to wonder whether his instructions with regard to the north room had been carried out.

He decided that, comfortable though the library was, it was worth while to go up to the passage and see whether the door of the north room was open and the fire lit. He was a determined man. He was really very much annoyed when he saw no gleam of light at the further end of the passage. Still, perhaps the door had swung to. He walked down the passage and tried it. It was locked.

Mr. Matthews seldom allowed his temper, which was a hot one, to get the better of him. He stood a moment, waiting for it to cool; and, as he paused in the dim corridor, he heard a faint sound. It was like a faint *thud*, as if some soft object had fallen to the ground; then came a very faint light rustling sliding sound.

He was almost sure that the sound came from the other side of the closed door. He thought perhaps the lock had merely stuck, and that Sharpe was within, closing windows or whatnot: but a second try at the door convinced him that it was locked fast. The sounds, then, must be an echo from some other part of the winding house. In any case, what really mattered was that his orders had been disobeyed.

He paid a visit to the Sharpes in the kitchen and made this quite clear.

The next morning, Wednesday, the sun rose apparently refreshed by the previous day's holiday. It was a magnificent day, with a sky of so deep and serene a blue that it seemed impossible that it could really have existed behind yesterday's rain. Mr. Matthews interviewed Sharpe and repeated his instructions with regard to the airing of all the rooms, irrespective of their history, aspect, or any other peculiarity. He thought it unlikely that he would be again disobeyed: and he was right, for chance visits to the meeting of the four passages always found a cool breeze blowing and showed four rows of open doors and glimpses of open windows.

In the afternoon the sun streamed out so invitingly that Mr. Matthews felt a desire to revisit his domain under these new conditions. He particularly wanted to see the effect of the golden light on the carved panelling of the north room, and to examine its design more closely.

This proved to be ordinary enough. There were plain panels reaching from the floor to a height of about three feet; then came a band of carving, ornament and scriptural texts intermingled; then twelve large panels, each four or five feet high. Each of these was surrounded by a frame of carved ornament, and they were separated from one another by narrower panels of plain wood. On the twelve panels were roughly carved twelve figures; and Mr. Matthews, noticing one with keys and another bearing an eagle, put them down as representations of the twelve apostles. All the carving was rough and amateurish, lacking the exquisite finish and proportion of skilled Tudor workmanship; yet Mr. Matthews felt little doubt in his mind that the curious designs, odd and archaic in conception, conventional to a degree, were of the sixteenth century.

"I'll get Mr. Molyneux up to have a look at them," he decided. "He'll know if they're fake or genuine antique."

An examination of the furniture yielded little beyond the bare wood of which they were made. Only in the desk did the American see anything at all interesting. This was a portrait – a rough but powerful sketch done on parchment; it was like a strong, though untaught, copy of a Dürer portrait; and yet it had the impress of originality.

It was the head of a man, apparently a priest, in the dress of the sixteenth century. The forehead was high and narrow, the cheeks sunken, the line of the jaw long and prominent. The mouth, thin-lipped and drooping, showed faintly through a straggling beard; the ears were singularly fine and sensitive. The eyes were so sunken under the overhanging, almost hairless, brows that it was difficult to see how the artist had managed to give them their expression of brooding horror. They were like the eyes of a haunted man.

Mr. Matthews felt strangely stirred by the portrait. He could hardly take his eyes from the fascinating, fascinated gaze of the picture.

"If it's not valuable, it ought to be," he muttered. "The thing looks alive! He might speak any minute – and I guess he'd have some pretty awful things to tell."

The light was fading now, and the American, wishing to study his find more carefully, carried it downstairs with him. As he examined the drawing by the newly-lit lamp, it occurred to him to look for a signature on the back of the portrait. There was, however, no mention of the artist; all he could see were words written in the crabbed and angular print often used in ecclesiastical documents of the period. "Dom: Hierime Lindalle: 1562. Eccles. XIV, 121," he read: and lower down two texts in full – "Have regard unto My Name; for it shalle be to thee for greate Treasures of golde. Eccles XLI, 15," and "And he finisht alle the worke that he didd in ye Hous of ye Lorde and browght in ye thinges that were Dedicated, ye Golde and ye Siluere and ye Vesells, and layd up ye Treasoure in ye House. 1 Kings VII, 51."

These did not interest Mr. Matthews greatly, and when he had studied the curious, painful drawing a little longer, he put it away. It was about nine that evening when, having nothing to do, he decided to get on with the sorting of some papers he intended to arrange in the form of a pamphlet on the Colour Question in the United States. They were in his bedroom, and he went up at once for them.

As he reached the head of the stairs he noticed Sharpe in the north passage. He could not quite see what he was doing; but he noticed that the door of the north room was shut.

"Sharpe," he said quietly, "have you just shut that door?"

The man jumped violently, and dropped, with a crash and a spatter of liquid, something that he had been carrying in his hand.

"What's that?" asked the American, his suspicions at once

aroused.

"It's — I-I've just been fillin' up the 'oly water stoups, sir," stammered Sharpe. "It's a thing we never leave undone, sir, and I'd nearly forgot it. They've been kep' filled ever since the 'ouse was built, so they say, and I promised Mr. Langtre as I would see to it."

The American bent down to the splash that spread right across the passage from wall to wall. It certainly had no scent. A glance assured him that the little receptacles on the walls had been recently filled.

"Right," he said, "and can you give me as good a reason for shutting that door? I said it was to be left open."

Sharpe muttered something by which he gave his employer to understand that he " 'adn't understood as the door was to be left open at night," that it didn't do the rooms no good, and that he hoped Mr. Matthews wouldn't insist. It was all very incoherent and very rapidly spoken, and the American again entertained doubts as to the man's *bona fides*: but he contented himself with repeating his orders to Sharpe to open the door of the north room, and standing to watch him do it.

The man went with infinite reluctance, like one walking to a torture chamber. He turned the key — Mr. Matthews noted grimly that the door was locked — and then, flinging open the door, fairly ran down the passage to the place where his employer stood awaiting him. He was white-lipped and shaking, and suddenly the American saw — the man was afraid! He had, of course, been brought up on village traditions of the haunted room, and he had intended to keep that door locked at all costs. Matthews half thought of reassuring him by going and relocking the door: but no, he wouldn't pander to these superstitions. He fetched his papers and spent a long evening in their classification and arrangement; then, happily conscious of time well spent, he went up to bed.

He woke once or twice in the night, and once thought he heard a faint scraping rustling sound, such as he had heard while waiting in the passage the day before. He listened intently, but heard nothing; and attributing the impression either to a dream or to the same natural cause that had occasioned it before, he curled up comfortably and went to sleep.

He woke vigorous and cheerful, full of the determination to call on Mr. Molyneux and ask him about the picture and the panels. He dressed with speed and energy, and went out of his room with happy anticipations of breakfast.

As he came out on the landing he noticed that the dark splash caused by the fallen holy water still stained the floor; and then he saw that another stain – a bright glistening trail – led from the open door of the north room to the splash on the floor.

It was the long slimy trail that a snail leaves, only it was quite unusually large. It was as if a slug or snail thirty or forty times bigger than the usual variety had crawled from the room along the passage until it came to the splash of water on the floor.

"Very curious," he thought. "I never knew before that slugs got up so high into a house. Thought it was the ground floor for theirs... By gosh!" he added, struck by an idea, "that was the sound I heard! Of course it was. But, my word, it must be some snail to make a noise you can hear! Only one trail, too."

After breakfast, Mr. Matthews decided that, raw and damp as the morning was, he would stroll down to the Vicarage with his newly-discovered picture: and he accordingly went, the portrait under his arm.

The Vicar was in, and pleased to see him. They exchanged civilities, and then Mr. Matthews, producing the portrait, broached the subject of his call.

"Well?" he asked, when the other had studied the drawing for some minutes in silence, "what do you think of it?"

"It's an extraordinary thing," said the Vicar slowly. "Quite unique, and, I should say, valuable. And yet, Mr. Matthews," he went on, taking off his *pince-nez* and laying down the picture, "if that portrait were mine, I declare to you I should burn it here and now. It is the picture of a fiend," he added with energy. "I consider it to be an unholy thing."

The American was considerably surprised at this outburst of fanatical superstition – for so he could not help thinking it – from a man as shy and reserved as the Vicar.

"Oh, come, sir," he said, laughing a little. "It's not as bad as that. It's odd, I admit, and it has a trick of haunting one; but after all the poor chap's dead, and I guess he had to pay for what he did."

"That's true," said the Vicar. Repugnance and antiquarian enthusiasm struggled within him as he picked up the drawing again.

"Oh, by the way," said Matthews, "I wanted to ask you about those texts on the back. What Book do they come from? I thought I knew my Bible tolerably well – New England, you know – but I don't just get the ones he's copied out."

The Vicar turned over the portrait and read the inscription.

"'Dom. Hierime Lindalle, 1562.' That would be about the year of his death," he remarked. "Then a text from Ecclesiasticus. Then here, lower down, another text from the same Book – 'Have regard unto My Name, for it shall be unto thee for a Treasure of gold.' Then a third, from the Book of Kings. It's not surprising you didn't recognise it, Mr. Matthews: Ecclesiasticus is an apocryphal Book, admitted by the Romans. It's not in the Anglican Bible at all. Still, the text from Kings doesn't strike me as quite accurate. Stay, I have the Latin Vulgate here somewhere."

He turned to his bookshelf.

"Here we are. Let's see, what's the first? Eccles, XIV, 121, copied just after the date."

"Will you translate?" asked the American. "Latin wasn't included in my schooling."

"Well, it's roughly this: 'Remember that death is not slow and the covenant of hell hath been shown to thee.' That was in the year of his death. No doubt the poor man, poring alone over his books and incantations, allowed the idea of his seven years' pact with the devil so to prey on his mind that he did in fact die in the given year."

"And left this as a kind of warning to other necromancers? I dare say you're right, sir. And the other reference, the one from Kings?"

Slowly the Vicar translated.

"'And he finished all the work that he did in the house of the Lord, and brought in the things that were dedicated, the gold and the silver and the vessels, and laid them up in the treasures of the house of the Lord.' He hasn't copied it accurately, you see. He has 'and laid up the treasure in the house.' And he has left out the reference to David."

"And what's the other from Eccle-what's-his-name?"

"That, again, is inaccurately copied," said the Vicar, turning over the leaves of his book. "It should be, 'Have regard to *thy* name: for it shall abide with thee for a great and precious treasure.'"

"It's queer, isn't it, that when he went to the trouble of copying out the whole texts he should have done it wrong? Say, Mr. Molyneux, I can't help sort of wondering—"

Their eyes met.

"The same thought occurred to me," said the Vicar quietly. "I believe the misquotations are intentional. I believe it's a clue to the place where he concealed the treasure – the stolen gold and jewelled plate of the chapel. You see," he went on with growing excitement, "the first of the misquoted texts concerns church vessels, and implies, or so I take it, that the plate was not melted down in his chemical experiments, but that he 'laid up the treasure in the house.'"

"That's what I make of it," said the American. "But the other one does me. Let's see: 'Have regard unto My Name, for it shall be unto thee for a treasure of gold.' Why, say, Vicar, that's it – the clue to the hiding-place is in the man's name!"

"I believe you're right!" cried the Vicar. "Some hint – perhaps a cipher—"

" 'Dom: Hierime Lindalle.' Hm. This needs some brain. Say, sir, what's wrong with you coming up to the Manor to lunch and working it out? We might find another clue in the room."

The Vicar agreed, and the two men set out for the Manor. They found a distinctly good meal awaiting them, and, after a quiet smoke, went up together to the north room.

"I guess Dom. Whats-his-name did these himself," said Mr. Matthews, looking round the rough carvings. "These gentlemen are the twelve apostles I take it. I'm going by Peter here," and he indicated the figure bearing a key.

"Yes, and that's St. John with the eagle; and St. Andrew with the

41

bread. Why, of course, they're rough copies of the apostles in the Langtre Psalter," he continued with increasing enthusiasm. "They are quite unique in design and conception, and in the Psalter each has a text attached. So against St. James, who is drawn as you see with his head half severed, is the text 'And James the brother of John he killed with the sword.' Each one can be identified in the same way. But *the* curiosity of the set is the representation of Judas: an extraordinary drawing, showing him falling out of the tree in which he is attempting to hang himself. You must see that."

And he began to make the circuit of the room.

"Pity the light is so bad," said Matthews. "I can only just see the figures. But I don't see one such as you describe."

"Neither do I," admitted the Vicar in some perplexity. "He has the Twelve, too."

"Perhaps Judas touched him a little too near," suggested the American. "He may count his twelve after the Acts."

"Let's see, said Mr Molyneux. "I ought to be able to identify them all from the Psalter."

He again went slowly round the room, murmuring the names of the apostles.

"Philip, Thomas with his finger outstretched; and this, with the book and the lion, of course is Mark. Now that's very odd," he said, turning to the American. "I wonder why he included Mark?"

"To make up the dozen, I guess," said Mr. Matthews. "After all, he was an evangelist, if he wasn't an apostle. Now, sir, before the light quite goes, let's just copy down these texts he has in the band round the wall, and then we'll see what we can make of 'em."

"The first," said the Vicar, "is Psalms cxx, 6 – 'The sun shall not smite it by day, nor the moon by night.'"

Mr. Matthews wrote rapidly.

"Next, just a reference – Ecclesiasticus xxxi, 7. Then St. Matthew vi, 21 – 'Where the treasure is, there will the heart be also.' Then another reference to Ecclesiasticus xxii, 12. That's all."

Matthews shut his notebook and slipped it into his pocket. Now we'll go down to the library and have a go at the puzzle," he said genially.

"Of course," said the Vicar as they descended the stairs, "that first text is another misquotation. In the Authorised Version, at any rate, the verse is 'The sun shall not smite *thee* by day.'"

"Why, you're right," said Matthews. "We'll just see what the Papists say. But it strikes me, sir, that any text that's copied in full is wrong and that's the clue."

In the library, established in armchairs, one with the paper of texts, the other with his Latin Vulgate, they traced out the references. The first was, as the Vicar had said, wrong.

"That don't tell us much," complained the American. "It applies to the treasure, I guess, but it's not much help to know that 'the sun will not smite it by day nor the moon by night.'"

"It may refer to the hiding place," said the Vicar. "That would suggest some hole or cellar or vault."

"That's so," admitted the American. "Now, Ecclesiasticus xxxi, 7."

The Vicar read aloud.

"'Gold is a stumbling block to them that sacrifice for it; woe to them that eagerly follow after it: every fool shall perish by it.' At once a lamentation and a warning from the dead devil-worshipper," he said. Then, with some hesitation, "Mr Matthews, it's evident the man had some horrible experience. Don't you think it would be wiser to abandon the search?"

"Abandon it, Vicar? What, when we're just getting on the track? Not if I know it," cried Matthews. "Why, this is just the biggest thrill that ever happened! And if there's any risk, why, that makes it all the better. Come on, what's next? Matthew vi, 21."

"That's from the Sermon on the Mount... Yes, I thought so. It really reads, 'Where *thy* treasure is, there shall *thy* heart be also.' Another deliberate misquotation."

"And the last? Ecclesiasticus again, xxii, 12."

The Vicar read it with a certain solemnity.

"'The wicked life of a wicked fool is worse than death.'"

"He certainly didn't get much hilarious pleasure out of the sacrilege," commented the American.

The Vicar said nothing. Somehow they both felt a little uncomfortable.

"Well, now, let's get down to work," said Matthews, throwing off his momentary discomfort. "We've got three clues. 'Have regard unto my name, for it shall be unto thee for a great treasure.' 'The sun shall not smite it by day nor the moon by night.' 'Where the treasure is, there shall the heart be also.' Let's get on to the name. 'Dom: Hierime Lindalle.' Now what's wrong with that as a name?"

They puzzled over this for some time, replacing letters by figures, rearranging the letters to form anagrams, seeking for some principle to guide them to the clue. Tea was served and eaten almost silently as the two men badgered their brains over the riddle of the priest's name.

At last the American looked up.

"No good," he said; and the Vicar shook his head.

" 'Hierime' strikes me as being a bit of a freak in the way of a name," commented Matthews. "Was he a saint?"

"Why, yes," said Mr. Molyneux. "Saint Hiereme, or Jerome, was a Father of the Church, a hermit who translated the Bible into Latin."

"Perhaps that accounts for this chap's attention to the text," suggested Matthews.

"Perhaps. St. Jerome was a great scholar. No doubt you know Dürer's famous pictures of him – in the desert, and at work in his room, with his lion at his feet."

"What's that?" cried the American. "A *lion*, did you say?"

"Why, yes, but–"

"What about that twelfth panel – the one with the book and the lion? What's the betting it's not Mark at all, but *Jerome*? The sly beggar! He slips in a figure he knows we'll take for Mark, and all the time–"

"I declare I believe you're right!" exclaimed Mr. Molyneux, flushed with excitement. "That's the clue – the panel in the north room."

"And, look here, the next fits," cried Matthews. " 'The sun shall not smite it by day nor the moon by night.' Do you remember just where that panel is? It's between the windows in the north wall. No direct light ever touches it."

"You're right!" cried the Vicar, almost as much excited as the American. "And the last clue – the heart?"

"This is where we go and look," declared Mr. Matthews.

The day was nearly ended, but a few rays of light struggled dimly into the north passage. As they hurried along, a small gleaming object lying on the floor met their eyes. Matthews stooped and picked it up. It was a thin silver chain to which was attached a tiny crucifix – a trinket such as is worn by a large majority of Catholics.

"One of the Sharpes dropped it, I reckon," said the American. "I'll take it down when I go." And he dropped it into his pocket.

In the north room the light had almost gone; but enough remained to direct the two men to the panel. "See here, the book *is* the Vulgate!" cried Matthews, peering closely at the carving. "We're right on the trail."

"'Where the treasure is, there the heart is also,'" murmured the Vicar. "Now, what can that mean?"

They tried the breast of the carved figure in all possible ways, with no result.

"Well, if that's not plumb annoying!" cried the American, pausing in his efforts. "I guess it must be another of his tricks. The wall's hollow here, too, I'd take my oath," and he rapped the panel with his knuckles. It certainly was not solid. It gave a queer echo, and Mr. Matthews thought he detected a faint sound, as of something stirring within the wall.

"Something moved!" he cried excitedly. "Guess it might've been machinery..." But further knockings produced no result.

"Let's try the decorated border," suggested Mr. Molyneux. "There may be some hint there."

The border was made up of wreaths of fruit and flowers, broken at intervals by shields so small that the quarterings were almost invisible. In some the arms could only be guessed from the crest, which was generally cut more deeply and with greater care than the shield.

"That's a queer crest," said Matthews, pointing to one of these. "Looks more like a setting sun than anything."

"I daresay it is," said the Vicar. "There was a lady of the Wigram family, whose crest is a rising sun, who intermarried with the Langtres. The arms are quite gone from the shield, though. It is perfectly smooth."

The light was now so bad that by common consent they abandoned their hunt till next day, and went down again to the lamp-lit library.

"Why, Mr. Molyneux, I'm afraid I've tired you by my treasure hunt," said Matthews, penitently, as he saw the Vicar's pale face.

"It's nothing – nothing at all," protested the other. "Just a little headache – my eyes are not strong. And I found that north room very close."

"You look as if bed was the place for you," declared Matthews; and the Vicar needed little urging, after dinner, to retire early. The American followed at eleven: not because he felt inclined for sleep, but because he wished to wake in the morning with a brain clear to tackle the problem of the panel. He was excited, and undressed with rapid, untidy movements, flinging down his discarded garments with utter disregard for neatness. The result of this was that his coat, thrown carelessly, fell upside-down, scattering the contents of the pockets over the floor. It was only then that he saw and remembered the silver chain and cross he had picked up.

"I must remember to give that back to the Sharpes," he thought. "Where'll I put it?" Then a queer fancy came into his head, and he slipped the chain round his neck.

"Guess I shan't forget it now," he chuckled, as he slid between the sheets.

The clocks had struck midnight, and still Mr. Matthews lay awake. The riddle of the panel bothered him. Try as he would, he could not see what the hint about the heart was intended to convey. He ran over the carving again and again in his mind – the draped figure with the book, the conventional lion beside it, placed on a perfectly plain background, and below it the thickly decorated border with its scrolls and shields.

He grew sleepy, and his thoughts began to stray. He thought of the chain, of Sharpe, of the holy-water stoups, of the shrine in the passage, of the many plaster statues about the house, and of one in particular that he had noticed in Mrs. Sharpe's room – a Christ with outstretched arms and a crimson heart emitting rays showing on the breast...

Mr. Matthews sat up, wide awake. That thing in the border that they had taken for a crested shield – that smooth triangle with the rays springing from it – it was not a shield at all: it represented a *heart*! He had solved the puzzle.

He leapt out of bed, armed himself with an electric torch, and fairly ran down the corridor to the north room. The single beam of light from his torch made the surrounding darkness seem almost opaque. In a dim subconscious way Matthews associated the dense gloom with the clammy, earthy smell that now seemed intensified; but he paid no conscious attention to either.

He walked with a quick, resolute stride to the panel, and soon found the smooth triangle in the decoration of the border. Of course, it was a heart – the conventional representation! He put his finger on it and pressed. He felt the panel slowly move.

He could not wait for it to swing fully open; he thrust his hand into the widening chink between the wall and the wood. There *was* something there, down in the bottom of the hole in the wall. Eagerly he reached for it.

It was piled up, and felt slimy to his touch. Then he dropped his torch with a hoarse cry; for, as he touched it, it moved, and a long slimy arm slid up his wrist.

Frantically he tore at his hand. He got it free for a second, and, turning, rushed to the door. He heard, as he ran, a heavy *flop*, and then a whispering, scratching sound. He knew that the thing had dropped from its lair and was dragging its loathsome length in pursuit. As he reached the door a tentacle, both slimy and hairy, curved round one ankle: another pawed at his left arm: and with a sickening thrill of disgust he felt something cold and slimy touch the back of his neck.

He gave a shriek of loathing and terror as he fell his length in the passage.

It was three weeks before Mr. Matthews, now installed at the Vicarage, could bring himself to speak of the end of that night. Then he asked, quite abruptly.

"How do you account for my escape, Molyneux? It – it was at my throat. I-I felt it..."

"One can't really account for any of these things," replied the Vicar, gravely. "Only – there is this. You had round your neck the image of Christ. I think the – thing – had touched it, for it – it was retreating when I heard you scream and came out. I-I saw it – dimly – and its trail... And I can't tell you how much I wished that I had read you a passage out of the manuscript about the room – a passage I left out. It might have warned you."

"Will you tell me now?"

"It describes the finding of the body of Job Harcott. It reads like this – I almost know it by heart since... since you so nearly..." He gulped, and then went on in grave tones –

"'We found him indeede in ye passage wh. leadeth to yt. accursed roome. He was Starke Naked and his Bodie fearsomelie swolne, longe Trayls of Slyme compassing him aboute as it were in a Nett.'"

CELUI-LÀ

"I DON'T for a moment expect you to take my advice," said Dr. Foster, looking shrewdly at his patient, "but I'll give it all the same. It's this. Pack a bag with a few things and go off tomorrow to some tiny seaside or mountain place, preferably out of England, so that you won't meet a soul you know. Live there absolutely quietly for three or four weeks, taking a reasonable amount of exercise, and then write and tell me that you're all right again."

"Easier said than done," growled Maddox. "There aren't any quiet places left that I know of, and if there were there wouldn't be any digs to be had at no notice."

Foster considered.

"I know the very thing," he cried suddenly. "There's a little place on the Breton coast – fishing village, very small and scattered, with a long stretch of beach, heath and moor inland, quiet as can be. I happen to know the curé there quite fairly well, and he's an extremely decent, homely little chap. Vétier his name is. He'd take you in. I'll write to him tonight."

After that, Maddox couldn't in decency hold out. Old Foster had been very good, really, over the whole thing; besides, it was nearly as much bother to fight him as it was to go. In less than a week Maddox was on his way to Kerouac.

Foster saw him off with relief. He knew Maddox well and knew that he was suffering from years of overwork and worry; he understood how very repugnant effort of any kind was to him

– or thought he did but in reality no one can quite understand the state of exasperation or depression that illness can produce in someone else. Yet as the absurd little train that Maddox took at Lamballe puffed serenely along between tiny rough orchards, the overwrought passenger began to feel soothed and then, as the line turned north and west and the cool wind came in from across the dim stretches of moorland, he grew content and almost serene.

Dusk had fallen when he got out at the shed that marked the station of Kerouac. The curé, a short, plump man, in soutane and broad-brimmed hat, met him with the kind, almost effusive, greeting that Breton peasants give to a guest, and conducted the stumbling steps of his visitor to a rough country lane falling steeply downhill between two high, dark banks that smelt of gorse and heather and damp earth. Maddox could just see the level line of sea lying before him framed by the steep banks of moor on either hand. Above a few pale stars glimmered in the dim sky. It was very peaceful.

Maddox fell into the simple life of the Kerouac presbytery at once. The curé was, as Foster had said, a very homely, friendly little man, always serene and nearly always busy, for he had a large and scattered flock and took a very real interest in the affairs of each member of it. Also, Maddox gathered, money was none too plentiful, for the curé did all the work of the church himself, even down to the trimming of the grass and shrubs that surrounded the little wind-swept building.

The country also appealed very strongly to the visitor. It was at once desolate and friendly, rough and peaceful. He particularly liked the long reaches of the shore, where the tangle of heath and whin gave place to tufts of coarse, whitish grass and then to a belt of shingle and the long level stretches of smooth sand. He liked to walk there when evening had fallen, the moorland on his left rising black to the grey sky, the sea, smooth and calm, stretching out infinitely on his right, a shining ripple lifting here and there. Oddly enough, M. le Curé did not seem to approve of these evening rambles; but that, Maddox told himself, was common among peasants of all races; and he idly wondered whether this were due to a natural liking for the fireside after a day in the open, or whether there were in it some ancient fear of the spirits and demons that country people used to fear in the dim time *entre le chien et le loup*. Anyhow, he wasn't going to give up his evening strolls for a superstition of someone else's!

It was near the end of October, but very calm weather for the time of year; and one evening the air was so mild and the faint shine of the stars so lovely that Maddox extended his walk beyond its usual limits. He had always had the beach to himself at that time of the evening and he felt a natural, if quite unjustifiable annoyance when he first noticed that there was someone else on the shore.

The figure was perhaps fifty yards away. At first he thought it was a peasant woman, for it had some sort of hood drawn over the head, and the arms, which it was waving or wringing, were covered by long, hanging sleeves. Then as he drew nearer, he saw that it was far too tall for a woman, and jumped to the conclusion that it must be a monk or wandering friar of quite exceptional height.

The light was very dim, for the new moon had set, and the stars showed a faint diffused light among thin drifts of cloud; but even so Maddox could not help noticing that the person before him was behaving very oddly. It – he could not determine the sex – moved at an incredible speed up and down a short stretch of beach waving its draped arms; then suddenly, to his horror, it broke out into a hideous cry, like the howl of a dog. There was something in that cry that turned Maddox cold. Again it rose, and again – an eerie, wailing, hooting sound, dying away over the empty moor. And then the creature dropped on its knees and began scratching at the sand with its hands. A memory, forgotten until now, flashed into Maddox's mind – a memory of that rather horrible story in Hans Andersen about Anne Lisbeth and the drowned child...

The thin cloud obscured the faint light for a moment. When Maddox looked again the figure was still crouching on the shore, scrabbling with its fingers in the loose sand; and this time it gave Maddox the impression of something else – a horrible impression of an enormous toad. He hesitated, and then swallowing down his reluctance with an effort, walked towards the crouching, shrouded figure.

As he approached it suddenly sprang upright, and with a curious, gliding movement, impossible to describe, sped away inland at an incredible speed, its gown flapping as it went. Again Maddox heard the longdrawn mournful howl.

Maddox stood gazing through the thickening dusk.

"Of course it's impossible to tell in this light," he muttered to himself, "but it certainly did look extraordinarily tall – and what an odd look it had of being *flat*. It looked like a scarecrow, with no thickness..."

He wondered at his own relief that the creature had gone. He told himself that it was because he loathed any abnormality, and there could be no doubt that the person he had seen, whether it were woman or monk, was crazed, if not quite insane.

He walked to the place where it had crouched. Yes, there was the patch of disturbed sand, rough among the surrounding smoothness. It occurred to him to look for the footprints made by the flying figure to see if they bore out his impression of abnormal height; but either the light was too bad for him to find them, or the creature had leapt straight on to the belt of shingle. At any rate, there were no footmarks visible.

Maddox knelt beside the patch of disturbed sand and half idly, half in interest, began himself to sift it through his fingers. He felt something hard and smooth – a stone perhaps? He took it up.

It was not a stone, anyhow, though the loose, damp sand clung to it so that he could not clearly distinguish what it was. He got to his feet, clearing it with his handkerchief; and then he saw that it was a box or case, three or four inches long, covered with some kind of rude carving. It fell open of itself as he turned it about, and he saw that inside was a wrapping of something like, yet unlike, leather; inside again was something that crackled like paper.

He looked round to see whether the figure that had either buried or sought this object – he was not sure which it had done – was returning; but he could see nothing but the bushes of gorse and heath black and stunted against the grey sky. There was no sound but the sigh of the night wind and the gentle lap of the incoming tide. His curiosity proved too strong for him, and he slipped the case into his pocket as he turned homewards.

Supper – a simple meal of soup and cheese and cider – was awaiting him when he got in, and he had no time to do more than change his shoes and wash his hands; but after supper, sitting on one side of the wide hearth while the curé smoked placidly on the other, Maddox felt the little box in his pocket, and began to tell his host of his queer adventure.

The curé's lack of enthusiasm rather damped him. No, he knew of no woman in the whole of his wide parish who would behave as Maddox described. There was no monastery in the neighbourhood, and if there were it would not be permitted to the brethren to act like that. He seemed mildly incredulous, in fact, until Maddox, quite nettled, took out the little case and slapped it down on the table.

It was a more uncommon object than he had at first supposed. It was, to begin with, extremely heavy and hard – as heavy as lead, but of a far harder metal. The chasing was queer; the figures reminded Maddox of runes; and remembering the prehistoric remains in Brittany, a thrill ran through him. He was no antiquarian but it occurred to him that this find of his might be an extremely interesting one.

He opened the case. As he had thought there was a scrap of some leathery substance within, carefully rolled round a piece of parchment. That couldn't be prehistoric of course; but Maddox was still interested. He smoothed it out and began stumblingly to read out the crabbed words. The language was Latin of a sort, and he was so occupied in endeavouring to make out the individual words that he made no attempt to construe their meaning until Father Vétier stopped him with a horrified cry and even tried to snatch the document out of his hand.

Maddox looked up exceedingly startled. The little priest was quite pale, and looked as horrified as if he had been asked to listen to the most shocking blasphemy.

"Why, *mon père*, what's wrong?" asked Maddox, astonished.

"You should not read things like that," panted the little curé. "It is wrong to have that paper. It is a great sin."

"Why? What does it mean? I wasn't translating."

A little colour crept back to the priest's cheeks, but he still looked greatly disturbed.

"It was an invocation," he whispered glancing over his shoulder. "It is a terrible paper, that. It calls up – *that one*."

Maddox's eyes grew bright and eager.

"Not really? Is it, honestly?" He opened out the sheet again.

The priest sprang to his feet.

"No, Monsieur, I must beg you! No! You have not understood–"

He looked so agitated that Maddox felt compunction. After all, the little chap had been very decent to him, and if he took it like that – ! But he couldn't help thinking that it was a pity to let these ignorant peasants have jobs as parish priests. Really, there was enough superstition in their church as it was without drafting old forgotten country charms and incantations into it. A little annoyed, he put the paper back into its case and dropped the whole thing into his pocket. He knew quite well that if the curé got his hands on it he would have no scruples whatever about destroying the whole thing.

That evening did not pass as pleasantly as usual. Maddox felt irritated by the crass ignorance of his companion, and Father Vétier was quite unlike his customary placid self. He seemed nervous, timid even; and Maddox noticed that when the presbytery cat sprang on to the back of her master's chair and rubbed her head silently against his ear, the curé almost sprang out of his seat as he hurriedly crossed himself. The time dragged until Maddox could propose retiring to bed; and long after he had been in his room he could hear Father Vétier (for the inner walls of the presbytery were mere lath and plaster) whispering prayers and clicking the beads of his rosary.

When morning came Maddox felt rather ashamed of himself for having alarmed the little priest, as he undoubtedly had done. His compunction increased when he saw Father Vétier as he came in from his early Mass, for the little man looked quite pale and downcast. Maddox mentally cursed himself. He felt like a man who has distressed a child, and he cast about for some small way of making amends. Halfway through déjeuner he had an idea.

"Father," he said, "you are making alterations in your church here, are you not?"

The little man brightened visibly. This, Maddox knew, was his pet hobby.

"But yes, Monsieur," he replied quite eagerly. "For some time now I have been at work, now that at last I have enough. Monseigneur has given me his blessing. It is, you see, that there is beside our church here the fragment of an old building – oh, but old! One says that perhaps it also was a church or a shrine once, but what do I know? – but it is very well built, very strong, and I conceived the idea that one might join it to the church. Figure to yourself, Monsieur, I should then have a double aisle! It will be magnificent. I shall paint it, naturally, to make all look as it should. The church is already painted of a blue of the most heavenly, for the Holy Virgin, with lilies in white – I had hoped for lilies of gold, but gold paint, it is incredible, the cost! – and the new chapel I will have in crimson for the Sacred Heart, with hearts of yellow as a border. It will be gay, isn't it?"

Maddox shuddered inwardly.

"Very gay," he agreed gloomily. There was something that appealed to him very much in the shabby whitewashed little church. He felt pained at the very thought of Father Vétier's blue and crimson and yellow. But the little curé noticed nothing.

"Already I have begun the present church," he babbled, "and, monsieur, you should see it! It is truly celestial, that colour. Now I shall begin to prepare the old building, so that as soon as the walls are built to join it to the present church, I can decorate. They will not take long, those little walls, not long at all, and then I shall paint..." He seemed lost in a vision of rapture. Maddox was both amused and touched. Good little chap, it had been a shame to annoy him over that silly incantation business. He felt a renewed impulse to please the friendly little man.

"Can I help you at all, Father?" he asked. "Could I scrape the walls for you or anything like that? I won't offer to paint; I'm not expert enough."

The priest positively beamed. He was a genial soul who loved company, even at his work; but even more he loved putting on thick layers of bright colours according to his long-planned design. To have a companion who did not wish to paint was more than he had ever hoped for. He accepted with delight.

After breakfast, Maddox was taken to see the proposed addition to the church. It stood on the north side of the little church (which, of course, ran east and west), and, as far as Maddox could see, consisted mainly of a piece of masonry running parallel with the wall of the church. Fragments of walls, now crumbled, almost joined it to the east and west ends of the north wall of the church; it might almost have been, at one time, a part of the little church. It certainly, as Father Vétier had said, would not take much alteration to connect it to the church as a north aisle. Maddox set to work to chip the plaster facing from the old wall with a good will.

In the afternoon the curé announced that he had to pay a visit to a sick man some miles away. He accepted with great gratitude his visitor's proposal that he should continue the preparations for the painting of the new aisle. With such efficient help, he said, he would have the addition to the church ready for the great feast of St. Michael, patron saint both of the village and the church. Maddox was delighted to see how completely his plan had worked in restoring the little man's placid good-humour.

Shortly after two, Maddox went into the churchyard and resumed his labours. He chipped away industriously, and was just beginning to find the work pall when he made a discovery that set him chipping again eagerly at the coat of plaster which later hands had daubed thickly on the original wall. There were undoubtedly mural paintings on the portion he had begun to uncover. Soon he had laid bare quite a large stretch, and could see that the decoration formed a band, six or seven feet deep, about two feet from the ground, nearly the whole length of the wall.

The light was fading, and the colours were dim, but Maddox could see enough to interest him extremely. The paintings seemed to represent a stretch of the seashore, and though the landscape was treated conventionally he thought it looked like part of the beach near Kerouac. There were figures in the painting, too; and these aroused his excitement, for one at least was familiar. It was a tall shape, hooded, with hanging draperies – the figure he had seen the night before on the beach. Perhaps it was due to the archaic treatment of the picture that this figure gave him the same impression of flatness. The other figure – if it was a figure – was even stranger. It crouched on the ground before the hooded shape, and to Maddox it suggested some rather disgusting animal – a toad or a thick, squat fish. The odd thing was that, although it squatted before the tall figure, it gave the impression of domination.

Maddox felt quite thrilled. He peered closely at the painting, endeavouring to make out clearly what it represented; but the short October afternoon was drawing in fast, and, beyond his first impression, he could gather very little. He noticed that there was one unexpected feature in the otherwise half-familiar landscape – a hillock or pile of large stones or rocks, on one side of which he could just make out words or fragments of words. *"Qui peuct venir"* he read in one place, and, lower down, *"Celuy qui ecoustera et qui viendra... sacri... mmes pendus..."*

There was also some vague object, a pile of seaweed, Maddox thought, lying heaped below the hillock.

Little though he knew either of art or of archaeology, Maddox was keenly interested by this discovery. He felt sure that this queer painting must represent some local legend or superstition. And it was very odd that he should have seen, or thought he had seen, that figure on the beach *before* he had discovered the mural painting. There could be no doubt that he had seen it; that it was no mere fancy of his tired mind there was the box and the incantation, or whatever it was, in his pocket to prove. And that gave him an idea. It would be extremely interesting if he should find that the old French words on the mural painting and the Latin words on the parchment in any way corresponded. He took the little metal case from his pocket and opened it.

"*'Clamabo et exaudiet me.'* 'I will call and he will hear.' That might be any prayer. Sounds rather like a psalm. *'Quoniam iste qui venire potest'* – ah! – *'qui peuct venir'!* – what's this? *'sacrificium hominum'* –

Heavens! *What's that?"*

Far off across the heath he heard a faint cry – the distant howling of the thing he had seen on the beach...

He listened intently. He could hear nothing more.

"Some dog howling," he said to himself. "I'm getting jumpy. Where was I?"

He turned back to the manuscript; but even during the few moments of distraction the light had faded, and he had to strain his eyes to see anything of the words.

" '*E paludinis ubi est habitaculum tuum ego te convoco*'," he read slowly aloud, spelling out the worn writing. "I don't think there's anything in the painting to correspond with that. How odd it is! 'From the marshes where thy dwelling is I call thee.' Why from the *marshes*, I wonder? '*E paludinis ubi est habitaculum tuum ego te convoco* –'."

He broke off abruptly. Again there came that dreadful howl – and it certainly was not the howl of a dog. It was quite close...

Maddox did not stop to consider. He leapt up, ran through the yard into the presbytery, and locked the door behind him. He went to the front door and locked that too; and he bolted every window in the tiny house. Then, and not till then, did he pause to wonder at his own precipitate flight. He was trembling violently, his breath coming in painful gasps. He told himself that he had acted like a hysterical old maid – like a schoolgirl. And yet he could not bring himself to open a window. He went into the little sitting-room and made up the fire to an unwonted size; then he tried to take an interest in Father Vétier's library of devotional books until the little curé himself should return. He was nervous and uneasy; it seemed to him that he could hear some creature (he told himself that it must be a large dog, or perhaps a goat) snuffling about the walls and under the door... He was inexpressibly relieved when at last he heard the short, decided step of the curé coming up the path to the house.

Maddox was restless that night. He had short, heavy snatches of sleep in which he was haunted by dreams of pursuit by that flat, hooded being; and once he woke with a strangled cry and a cold shudder of disgust from a dream that, in his flight, he had stumbled and fallen face downwards on something soft and cold which moved beneath him – a mass of toads... He lay awake for a long time after that dream; but he eventually slipped into a drowsy state, half waking and half sleeping, in which he had an uncomfortable impression that he was not alone in the room – that something was breathing close beside him, moving about in a fumbling, stealthy way. And his nerves were so overwrought that he simply had not the courage to put out a hand and feel for the matches lest his fingers should close on – something else. He did not try to imagine what.

Towards dawn he fell into an uneasy doze, and awoke with a start. Some sound had awakened him – a melancholy howling cry rang in his ears; but whether it had actually sounded or whether it was part of his memories and evil dreams he could not tell.

He looked ill and worn at breakfast, and gave his bad night as an excuse for failing to continue his work on the old wall. He spent a wretched, moping day; he could settle to nothing indoors.

At last, tempted by the mellow October sun, he decided to go for a brisk, short walk. He would return before dusk – he was quite firm about that – and he would avoid the lonely reaches of the shore.

The afternoon was delicious. The rich scent of the gorse and heather, warm in the sun, and the cool touch from the sea that just freshened the breeze, soothed and calmed Maddox wonderfully. He had almost forgotten his terrors of the night before – at least, he was able to push them into a back corner of his mind. He turned homewards contentedly – even in his new calm he was not going to be out after sundown – when his eyes happened to fall on the white road where the declining sun threw his shadow, long and thin, before him. As he saw that shadow, his heart gave a sudden heavy *thud*; for a second shadow walked beside his own.

He spun round. No mortal creature was in sight. The road stretched empty behind him, and on either hand the moorland spread its breast to the wide sky. He ran to the presbytery like a hunted thing.

That evening Father Vétier ventured to speak to him.

"Monsieur," he said, rather timidly, "I do not wish to intrude myself into your affairs. That understands itself. But I have promised my very good friend M. Foster that I will take care of you. You are not a Catholic, I know; but – will you wear this?"

As he spoke he took from his own neck a thin silver chain to which was attached a little medal, black with age, and held it out to his guest.

"Thank you, father," said Maddox simply, slipping the chain about his neck.

"Ah! That is well," said the little curé with satisfaction. "And now, monsieur, I venture to ask you – will you let me change your room? I have one, not as good as yours, I admit it, but which has in it a small opening into the church. You will perhaps repose yourself better there. You will permit?"

"With the greatest pleasure," said Maddox fervently. "You are very kind to me, father."

The little man patted his hand.

"It is that I like you very much, monsieur," he said naively. "And – I am not altogether a fool. We of Brittany see much that we do not look at, and hear much to which we do not listen."

"Father," said Maddox awkwardly, "I want to ask you something. When I began to read out that paper – you remember? –" (The curé nodded uneasily) – "you said that it was an invocation – that it summoned *celui-là*. Did you mean – the devil?"

"No, my son. I-I cannot tell you; It has no name with us of Kerouac. We say, simply, *celui-là*. You will not, if you please, speak of it again. It is not good to speak of it."

"No, I can imagine it isn't," said Maddox; and the conversation dropped. Maddox certainly slept better that night. In the morning he told himself that this might be for more than one reason. The bed might be more comfortable (but he knew it was not that); or he might have overtired himself the day before, or the little curé's offerings might somehow have given him a kind of impression of safety and protection without really having the least power to guard him. His feeling of security increased when the priest announced:

"Tomorrow we have another guest, monsieur. M. Foster has done me the honour to accept my invitation for a visit."

"Foster? Really? Excellent," cried Maddox. He felt that the doctor stood for science and civilisation and sanity and all the comfortable reassuring things of life that were so utterly lacking in the desolate wildness of Kerouac. Sure enough Foster came next day, and was just as stolid and ugly and completely reassuring as Maddox had hoped he would be and half feared he would not. He seemed to be ignoring his friend's physical condition at first, but on the day after his arrival he got to business.

"Maddox, I don't know how you expect to get fit again," he said. "You came here for the air as much as anything. I said you were to take moderate exercise. Yet here you stick moping about this poky little house." (Needless to say Father Vétier was not present when this conversation took place.) "What's wrong with the place, eh? I'd have said it was excellent walking country."

Maddox flushed a little. "It's a bit boring, walking alone," he said evasively, well aware that "boring" was not the right word.

"Perhaps... Yes. But you can get out a bit more now I'm here to come along. You might take me out this afternoon; the curé's going off to some kind of conference."

Maddox wondered uneasily how much Foster knew. Had he come by chance, off his own bat? Or had Father Vétier been worried about his first guest and sent for him? If that were so, what exactly had the priest said? He thought he'd soon get that out of Foster.

They walked along the beach, farther than Maddox had yet been. He had avoided the shore of late, and he had not felt up to going so far when he first came to Kerouac; yet, though he knew he had never been on that particular reach of shore, the place seemed familiar. It is, of course, a common thing to feel that one knows a place which one is now seeing for the first time; but the impression was so extremely vivid that Maddox couldn't help remarking on it to his companion.

"Rot, my dear man," said Foster bluntly. "You haven't been in Brittany before, and you say you've never been as far as this. It's not such uncommon country, you know; it's like lots of other places."

"I know," said Maddox; but he was not satisfied. He was poor company for the rest of the walk, and was very silent on the way home. No amount of chaff from Foster could rouse him, and at last the doctor abandoned the effort. The men reached the presbytery in silence.

The next day was close, threatening rain, though the downpour held off from hour to hour. Neither of the two Englishmen felt inclined to walk under that lowering sky. Father Vétier had a second urgent summons from his sick parishioner at Cap Morel, and set off, wrapped in a curious garment of tarpaulin, soon after the second déjeuner. He remarked that he might take the occasion of being so near to Prénoeuf to pay some visits there, and that he probably would not be in until nightfall.

"If monsieur should feel disposed," he said rather shyly to Maddox before he left, "M. Foster might be interested to see the alterations I propose for the church. He has taste, M. Foster. It might amuse him..."

He was so clearly keen to display his decorations, and yet a little afraid of appearing vain if he showed them himself, that Maddox smiled.

"I'm sure he'd like to see them," he said gently.

Yet, though he could have given no possible reason for it, he felt strongly disinclined to go near that half-ruined wall with its stretch of painting only half displayed. He knew it was absurd. He had worked there till he was tired; he had been startled by the howling of a dog. That was all. No doubt, when he came to look at it again, he would find that the fresco was the merest clumsy daub, and that his own overwrought nerves, together with the uncanny light of the gloaming and the beastly dog, had exaggerated it into something sinister and horrible. He declared to himself that if he had the courage to go and look again, he would simply laugh at himself and his terrors. But at the back of his mind he knew that he would never have gone alone; and it was a mixture of bravado and a kind of hope that Foster's horse-sense would lay his terror for him that finally induced him to propose a visit to the place.

Foster was interested, mildly, by what Maddox told him of the painting on the ruined wall. He went out first to the rough little churchyard; Maddox, half reluctantly, went to fetch down the little case he had picked up on the beach in order that Foster might with his own eyes compare the two inscriptions; and when he did go out to join his friend he could hardly bring himself to go over to the wall he had worked on. It took quite an effort to force his feet over to it.

The decoration was not quite as he had remembered it. The figures were so indistinct and faint that they were hardly visible. In fact, Maddox could well believe that a stranger would not recognise the daub as representing figures at all. His relief at this discovery was quite absurd. He felt as if an immense and crushing weight had been lifted from his spirit; and, his first anxiety over, he bent to examine the rest of the painting more attentively. That was nearly exactly as he remembered it – the pile of stones with the half-illegible words; the tumbled huddle of seaweed or rags lying before it; the long reach of shore – ah! that was it!

"Foster! Come and look here," he said.

"Where?" asked the doctor, strolling over.

"Look – this fresco or whatever it is. I said that bit of shore we saw yesterday was familiar. This is where I saw it."

"Mmmm. Might be... All very much alike, though, this part of the beach. I don't see anything to get worked up about."

"Oh! If you're going to take that line!" cried Maddox, exasperated. "You doctors are all alike – 'Keep calm' – 'Don't get excited' – 'Nothing to worry about'!..."

He broke off, gulping with sheer rage.

"My dear Maddox!" said Foster, startled by his silent friend's outburst. "I'm awfully sorry. I wasn't trying to snub you in the least. I simply thought–" He too broke off. Then he decided to risk another annoyance. "What have you got on your mind?" he asked, rather urgently. "Tell me, Maddox, there's a good chap. What is it?"

He paused hopefully; but Maddox had dried up. He could not explain. He knew that his solid, comfortable friend would never, *could* never understand that his terror was not imaginary; he could not bear to watch him soothing down his friend, to see the thought "hysteria" in his mind... Yet it would be a relief to tell...

"Look at this," he said at last. He took from his pocket the case he had found on the beach. "What do you make of that paper?" he asked.

Foster moved out of the shadow of the wall so that the pale, watery sunlight, struggling through the clouds, fell on the parchment. Maddox, a little relieved by the serious way he took it, turned back to examine the painting again. It was certainly very odd that the figures, which he remembered so clearly and which had seemed so very distinct, should now appear so dim that he doubted their reality. They seemed even fainter now than they had when he had looked at them a few minutes ago. And that heap flung beneath the hillock – what did that represent? He began to wonder whether that, too, were a figure – a drowned man, perhaps. He bent closer, and, as he stooped, he was aware that someone beside him was looking over his shoulder, almost leaning on him.

"Odd, Foster, isn't it?" he said. "What do you make of that huddled thing under the stones?"

There was no answer, and Maddox turned. Then he sprang to his feet with a shuddering cry that died in his throat. The thing so close to him was not his friend. It was the hooded creature of the beach...

Foster found the parchment so interesting that he was anxious to see it more clearly. He peered at it closely for a minute, and then decided to go into the presbytery for a light. He had some difficulty with the old-fashioned oil lamp; but when he finally got it burning he thought that the document fully repaid his trouble. He became so absorbed that it was not for some minutes that he realised that it was growing very dark and that Maddox had not yet come in. He felt quite disproportionately anxious as he hurried out to the tiny overgrown churchyard.

He was startled into something very like panic when he found no one there. Without reason, he knew that there was something horribly wrong and, blindly obeying the same instinct, he rushed out of the tiny enclosure and ran at his top speed down to the beach. He knew that he would find whatever there was to find on that lonely reach that was pictured on the old wall.

There was a faint glimmer of daylight still – enough to confuse the light until Foster, half distraught with a nameless fear, could hardly tell substance from shadow. But once he thought he saw ahead of him two figures – one a man's, and the other a tall wavering shape almost indistinguishable in the gloom.

The sand dragged at his feet till they felt like lead. He struggled on, his breath coming in gasps that tore his lungs. Then, at last, the sand gave way to coarse grass and then to a stretch of salt marshland, where the mud oozed up over his shoes and water came lapping about his ankles. Open pools lay here and there, and he saw, as he struggled and tore his feet from the viscous slime, horrible creatures like toads or thick, squat fish, moving heavily in the watery ooze.

The light had almost gone as he reached the line of beach he knew, and for one terrible moment he thought he was too late. There was the pile of stones; beneath them lay a huddled black mass. Something – was it a shadow? – wavered, tall and vague, above the heap, and before it squatted a shape that turned Foster cold – something thick, lumpish, like an enormous toad...

He screamed as he dragged his feet from the loathsome mud that clooped and gulped under him – screamed aloud for help...

Then suddenly he heard a voice – a human voice.

"*In nomine Dei Omnipotenti...*" it cried.

Foster made one stupendous effort, and fell forward on his knees. The blood sang in his ears, but through the hammering of his pulse he heard a sound like the howling of a dog dying away in the distance.

"It was by the providence of the good God that I was there," said Father Vétier afterwards. I do not often come by the shore – we of Kerouac, monsieur, we do not like the shore after it is dusk. But it was late, and the road by the shore is quicker. Indeed I think the good saints led me... But if my fear had been stronger so that I had not gone that way – and it was very strong, monsieur – I do not think that your friend would be living now."

"Nor do I," said Foster soberly. "My God, Father, it – it was nearly over. *Sacrificium hominum*, that beastly paper said... I-I saw the loathsome thing waiting... He was lying in front of that hellish altar or whatever it was... *Why*, Father? Why did it have that power over him?"

"I think it was that he read the – the invocation – aloud," said the curé slowly. "He called it, do you see, monsieur – he said the words. What he saw at first is – is often seen. We are used to it, we of Kerouac. We call it *Celui-là*. But it is, I believe, only a servant of – that other..."

"Well," said Foster soberly, "you're a brave man, Padre. I wouldn't spend an hour here if I could help it. As soon as poor Maddox can travel I'm going home with him. As to living here alone–!"

"And you are right to go," said Father Vétier, gravely. "But for me – no, monsieur. It is my post, do you see. And one prays, monsieur – one prays always."

THE ROOM

"You all agree, then?" asked Massingham, looking round at his guests.

"Quite, quite," said young Grindley of Brasenose.

"I am ready to fall in," said the Parson.

Vernon merely grunted. Really, after a dinner like that, it was a beastly shame to chatter.

"I'll do it, of course," said Reece, the tubby little curate whom Massingham had invited more out of cussedness than anything.

"All right, then. Mind, I don't guarantee that there is a ghost. I'm only going on local gossip and the fact that it's so damned hard to get any servants. And the house-agents, of course."

"You don't mean to say that *they* admit there's a ghost?" asked Ladislaw.

"No," grinned Massingham; "I'm going by what they didn't say... By the way, are you coming in, Mac?"

Ladislaw flushed.

"I – of course I will, if that's part of the bargain," he said a little doubtfully.

"My dear chap," drawled Grindley, "surely – I mean, I know people who think there's something in it and that, but *surely* – ?"

"I don't know," blurted Ladislaw. "Oh well, of course no one believes in the white-sheet-and-clanking-chains ghost; but – no, perhaps there aren't any in England," he ended abruptly.

They shouted with laughter. Ladislaw had in him the blood of generations of Highlanders, fanatical in their isolation and pride. Ladislaw grinned shamefacedly. He knew – well, perhaps he knew more than the others.

"Well, since we're all agreed," said Massingham briskly, "the next thing to do is to draw lots as to the order we go in. And look here," he added, reddening a little, "if anyone feels, when it comes to the point, that – that he'd rather drop it, you know, we'd – well, nobody'd think the worse of him." He looked round a little shamefacedly. "I don't want any nervous wrecks on my conscience," he added with a half-laugh.

Everybody smiled in his own individual fashion – Grindley just a trite superior, Ladislaw sympathetic, the Parson very kind and indulgent, Vernon bored, and Reece with the spontaneity of a child. Massingham, his duty done, looked relieved.

"Let's draw, then," he said. "I'll put all our names in this" – he tipped out the cigars from the box – "and numbers from one to – let's see – six, in this." He took a clean tumbler off the tray. Then he drew out his pocket-book and tore out two leaves which he again tore, each into six pieces. On one set he wrote numbers, on the other names. Then, folding up the scraps, he dropped one set into the box and the other into the tumbler.

"Now, let's see – Reece, you're the most transparently honest. You draw."

Reece jogged his chair up, his face beaming like a small boy at a conjuring show.

"What do I do?" he asked eagerly.

"You take one paper out of the box and another out of the glass and open them."

Reece obeyed.

"Amory," he said, opening one – "three."

The Parson smiled, still indulgent. "So two of you experience the ghost before I do," he said.

Reece went on with the drawing.

"Ladislaw – four," he said. "Grindley – one."

"Good old Grindley!" "Do down the spook, Grinders!" "Leave some for me!" vociferated the crowd, now thoroughly aroused.

"Reece – six. Uh, I did hope I'd be fairly early! Never mind. Vernon – two. Massingham – five. That's all." Reece beamed round on the company, polishing his circular steel-rimmed spectacles, rosy with excitement.

"Then I take it the order is Grindley, Vernon, myself, Ladislaw, Massingham, Reece," said the Parson. "Upon my word, I hope something will come of it. I rather envy you, Grindley – and you, Reece." Then he drew Reece a little aside. "I mean to exorcise anything I see," he said in a low voice. "Did you think of doing that? I'm quite willing to come last if – if the others really want to find out if they can see anything."

"Just as you like," said Reece. "But won't your exorcism have a better chance of proof if you try it on somewhere in the middle? I mean, say Grindley and Vernon – er – see something, and Ladislaw and Massingham and I don't–"

"Yes, you're right," said Amory, with more animation than usual. "It's best as it is. It's a clearer proof of the truth. Yes, Reece, you're quite right. Thank you."

His eyes had a curious gleam – the light of the fanatic, eager, bright and hard – in them.

"Lord! I pity the poor ghost when Amory once gets going," said Vernon with a short laugh. "I shouldn't like to be up against you when you were really mad, old man."

"Oh, come!" said Amory, flushing a little, with a rather shamefaced laugh. "It's only when I'm sure that I'm face to face with something really evil that I get angry. Then, I admit, I'm – er –"

"Implacable," put in Grindley. "It's most extraordinary," he went on, "how people seem to take a pride in certain of their – well, faults. Look at Massingham, now: he's got an absolute devil of a temper – I wouldn't answer for the safety of anyone who roused him – but I don't mind betting that he'll not only own to it, but be quite proud of it."

"Eh, What's that?" asked Massingham from the sideboard. "What's that about me?"

"Isn't it true that you're rather hot-tempered?" drawled Grindley.

"Got a brute of a temper," answered Massingham cheerfully.

"'Fact, when I do get going, I absolutely see red." He turned back to the syphon.

Grindley smiled faintly.

"I believe anger and pride are deadly sins, aren't they, Amory? – and no one minds owning to 'em; in fact, most people rather like being accused of 'em. But if I were to say that Vernon was a greedy sensualist, or that you, Amory, were the most damnably narrow, uncharitable brute I'd ever met, you'd be quite annoyed. Here's an example, now," went on the youthful moralist. "You know that pretty maid Lily who used to wait at dinner? What's become of her?"

"Left," growled Massingham. "She – er – well, *you* know. Pity, too, for I don't think she was a real bad 'un. Pretty girls don't stand much chance in country villages."

"Exactly," said Grindley. "It wasn't, probably, her fault at all, if you can call it a fault to follow the dictates of Nature; yet she gets kicked downhill by the likes of us."

"Really, Grindley," said Amory, his thin face pale, "I know its the fashion to be cynical about these things, but I consider it most immoral to take any but the strongest views on such a subject. If I had my way I should so deal with these cases as to prevent effectually their ever occurring again."

"Oh, come now, Amory!" broke in Vernon. "The cart-tail and whipping-post, eh? Damn it all, man, it's nature! Why, even in the Bible isn't there a woman – a real bad lot, too – who – er – got let off, don't you know?"

"If you mean the eighth chapter of St. John's Gospel," said Amory coldly, "most critics agree that it's not authentic. I believe the Romans admit it to be an interpolation. And in any case, there was no condoning of the crime: the woman was told to 'sin no more,' not that it was 'natural' and therefore not worthy of blame."

"Oh, well," yawned Vernon, "we all know that it's you Christians who go in for whips and tortures and burnings alive. Poor degraded sensualists like myself believe in the motto 'Live and let live.'"

Amory opened his mouth for an indignant reply, but Massingham cut in.

"I suppose we all show up on a question of that kind," he said, philosophically. "Amory'd do anything – anything at all – to punish transgressors – eh, Amory?"

The Parson nodded. "Old Vernon says 'Let 'em, if they want to. It don't hurt anyone else.' (Please stop me if I'm misjudging anyone.) Grindley says 'It's below me, of course, vulgar and that: but I believe it's natural, like over-eating or getting drunk.' I – well, I dislike the whole thing thoroughly, but I can't help thinking it's a necessary evil. As for Ladislaw, I don't believe he even knows it exists, or if he does he's so disgusted he shuts it out of his existence. Reece – I'm blessed if I know what Reece thinks."

"I think," said Reece, very pink and hot, and stammering in his confusion, "that it's a horrible thing, like d-deformity, that we are responsible for, just as we are for c-consumption or drink. It's b-beastly, but it's our f-fault, and we've got to s-stop it. And I'm af-fraid I don't quite agree with you, Amory, that p-punishment stops it. It's d-decency in people's lives that *p-prevents* it. And we've got to see that they have a chance to – well, to live c-clean. I say, I'm sorry. I didn't mean to jaw like that."

He collapsed into a deep armchair.

Grindley yawned.

"I'd no idea I'd uncork such deep vials of emotion and opinion," he said in his most irritating voice. "Shall we chuck it?" He lit a cigarette. "By-the-way, Masser, I suppose the – er – experiment begins tonight?"

"Just as you like," said Massingham. "It's your look-out, since you're the first on the list."

"Oh, well, I'll begin at once," said Grindley, rising. "I only hope they've made me up a decent bed. I believe that's really why people can't sleep in haunted rooms – maids won't take any trouble with the beds. Goodnight, you men."

"'Night, old chap." "Mind you have a good yarn for us tomorrow night." "Don't sleep right through the show, lazy swine." "Call out if you're frightened."

And so young Oxford went up to encounter the spirits of all time.

"If it wasn't that I'd promised," said Grindley next evening, with an abruptness strange to him, "I'd never say a word. And, mind, it isn't what you expect, any of you. I didn't see a thing."

His eyes, flickering and dark in his white face, glanced nervously round the group of men. He passed his tongue rapidly over his lips.

"But – something happened?" asked Vernon.

"Yes – oh yes! Something happened all right. But what it was I don't know – a dream, or a vision, or – an incarnation."

They looked at him intently. Could this nervous boy be the calm and slightly superior Grindley who had talked so fluently and well of the power of the trained intellect?

"P'raps once I tell you I'll get over it a bit," he broke out at last. "I think – I'm – possessed. No, I mean it absolutely literally. I never guessed before what it meant...

"I didn't take long over going to bed. It's a pleasant enough room, you know, and I was a bit sleepy after the warmth and the talking and that, and I never for a moment thought I'd be disturbed. If I'd known, nothing in this world – or the next – would ever have persuaded me to sleep in that cursed – yes, I mean it, *cursed* – room."

He paused a moment, trying to recover some of his wonted calm.

"Well, I went to bed, and, I suppose, to sleep. I never before quite understood what Hamlet meant about the dreams that might come when you're lying in the grave, dead. I thought I did, but I didn't. And he only guessed what the dreams of death might be. I *know*...

"I don't mean you to think that I just had a bad dream. I quite literally *became someone else* – in every nerve of my body, in every thought of my mind – yes, and in every secret wish of my heart. I knew myself intimately. I was myself in another incarnation, older, stronger, freer, nearer to elemental things, but still myself... I wish I could make you understand!" He broke off abruptly, and as abruptly resumed:

"Of course you all know the story of Dr. Faustus. It's a fine, dramatic story, you think, and Marlowe made a glorious, marvellous poem of it. You don't know – thank God every day of your lives that you don't know – what a fearful story it is. I do know. Last night – and God only knows how long before – I *was* that man."

He gulped.

"I-I'd done it, you know. I'd abandoned all goodness: I'd made my intellect, *mine*, my God, and worshipped it. I'd blasphemed, and – I had sold my soul.

"I can't attempt to tell you what it was like. You couldn't ever imagine it if you hadn't felt it. I was terrified at what I'd done. I was the living home of everything evil – I tell you, I was evil through and through, as if some fearful vapour had surrounded and soaked me. And – I was *afraid*. I tried to pray, and I knew it was hopeless. How could I hope to be heard? Oh, it's easy to talk of Despair – you don't know, you can never guess, what it is! I fought and struggled. I began broken prayers, and abandoned them at the first word, knowing I couldn't pray...

"I can't tell you how long it lasted. I lived a whole spiritual life through. No words can tell you what it was – it was a living hell, and it's – it's heaven to be awake."

"Grindley, old chap," said Reece softly, "it-it wasn't *you*, you know. It was some evil outside of you. It wasn't the real you."

Grindley turned a haggard face.

"It was – a possible me. I might have been – I nearly was – just that, blasphemous, hopeless. But – I know in time... I'm going out," he added abruptly. "Reece, will you come?"

Reece rose – Reece, on whom Grindley had often exercised a pretty wit; Reece the plain, the stupid, the comical and the kindly; and, without a word, they set out together.

The others lit pipes and cigarettes, poked the fire, mixed drinks; they breathed more freely.

"'Pon my word," said Vernon between puffs, "I'd no idea Grindley was such a kid. Expect he was horribly jumpy the whole time. Poor kid, he's beastly upset! And all about a dream!"

"Well, but it must have been a horribly vivid and peculiarly beastly dream," said Massingham. "He looks quite changed. Poor old Grindley!"

"Why 'poor'?" asked Ladislaw. "I call him lucky."

"*Lucky!*" exclaimed two or three of the others. And "How d'you make that out?" asked Vernon.

"Well – he knows in time. He's warned. It *was* in him, you know – that ambition and pride of intellect. Well – he's cured."

"Want to back out, Vernon?" asked Massingham, grinning. "Your shot tonight, you know. Don't think there's much chance of your letting your ambition and intellect sell *your* soul to the devil, you lazy swine. You'll sell it another way."

Vernon grinned blandly.

"If the bed's warm and comfortable I'll be all right, thanks," he yawned. "Don't mind how soon I get off, either. Say goodnight to the others for me, will you?"

He rose, stretching his arms, a fine figure of a man, verging on the corpulent, a little spoilt by good living, but handsome still.

It was very late when Grindley and Reece returned. They went upstairs, still together.

Everyone noticed how odd Vernon looked at breakfast. He did not look terrified and – yes, possessed – like Grindley; he looked like a man who has been brought face to face with some disgusting sight – white and shaken and sick. He ate nothing; he sat and crumbled bread with trembling fingers, and every now and then he would lift his eyes and look at one or another of them in a queer appealing way, as if he were guilty of some sin, and sorry for it, and his friends were his judges.

Everybody was a little uncomfortable and ill at ease: it was so odd to see Vernon, the debonair and confident Vernon, so piteously shaken. Breakfast was a hasty meal, for everyone was anxious to get it over and escape from those troubled questioning eyes.

But as chairs were pushed back and pipes lighted, Vernon suddenly spoke.

"I'm not going to make any story for you chaps tonight," he said abruptly. "There isn't one – for you. Yes, I've seen something. And I shan't forget what I've seen, as long as I live." Sweat started out on his forehead. "I'm not going to try and tell you what it was," he went on jerkily. "I'd as soon try to describe the most loathsome surgical operation or the most indecent physical illness. And if I wanted to, I couldn't. Thank Heaven, we haven't made the words for what I saw."

Eyes met startled eyes over the untidy table. It was mad, the whole business – a ghost hinted at while the remains of breakfast still littered the table; Vernon, of all people, confused, ashamed, disgusted, and – yes – penitent.

"Grindley was right," said Vernon heavily; "that place is cursed. And he's right, too, when he says that no one who hasn't tried can even guess what evil it puts into your mind, and how it brings out the vile things you have in your own soul. Only I'd rather have had his – dream, or incarnation, or whatever it was, than –"

There was silence in the room. Suddenly Vernon stood up. Involuntarily everyone looked at him – at the handsome face, now tormented with a kind of passion of disgust and remorse, at the haunted eyes that used to be so gay.

"I'm-I'm not so bad as that yet!" he cried with a sound like a sob, and left them sitting there.

Grindley rose, and soon was seen passing the window, making for the stables. Ladislaw sat with bowed head, contemplating his plate. Reece and Amory murmured together, and Massingham caught the words "holy water." He got up and went across to them.

"I say, you men, shall we drop it?" he asked. He was quite pale. "Grindley's collapse didn't altogether surprise me, but when poor old Vernon gets bowled over like this it's too much of a good thing. He looks ghastly. I didn't think he had it in him to feel like that."

The others glanced at one another.

"There must be some – well, influence or something – in that room," Massingham continued. "Something pretty awful, too. And I don't want anybody to go in there just out of bravado and get – well, damaged."

"I agree," said the Parson gravely, "that there must be something evil in that room. It's not contrary to dogma to believe that some places are soaked, as it were, in evil influence. But that's all the more reason, Massingham, for me to spend the night there. If exorcism and prayer can lay your ghost, I promise you it shall be laid."

"I know you're not afraid," said Massingham. "I'll admit that in a way it's your job. But, Amory, you know that young Grindley wasn't just a frightened kid last night. Something *had* happened to him – something pretty awful. And God only knows what it can have been that poor old Vernon saw. He's horrified – and I should have said that no god or devil could horrify Vernon."

"Whatever it is," said Amory steadily – "and I don't think we can deny that there is something – it's not stronger, nor half as strong, as the Powers that will be on my side. I am going into that room tonight, Massingham, convinced that there is in it some shocking evil, and equally convinced that I shall overcome it. It cannot withstand the minister of God."

Massingham flushed, as some men do when asked to talk familiarly of God. He preferred to speak of Providence.

"Well, Amory, you know best," he said. "Do as you think right. Only, for Heaven's sake, if you feel the smallest reluctance when it comes to the point, do chuck it! Swear you will."

"I am going to lay that spirit," said the Parson, steadily as ever, with a set mouth and a light in his eyes that warned Massingham that remonstrance was useless. He shrugged his shoulders.

"It's a pity you weren't born in the days of martyrs, Amory," he remarked. "You'd have enjoyed going to the stake for your principles."

Amory said nothing. Perhaps it was as well.

There was an unusual silence in the smoking-room that night. Grindley had been out in the wind and rain all day, and looked more his normal self though there was an odd hesitation in his manner and dread still lurked in his eyes. He glanced over his shoulder often, like a man who fears a horrible presence at his elbow; and he kept close to Reece. Vernon sat, his head sunk between his shoulders, staring sombrely at the fire. No one knew where he had been all that long and dreary day. The Parson sat apart, reading with moving lips, a look of exaltation on his face. Ladislaw and Massingham made an idle pretence at talk.

Suddenly Amory rose.

"Good-night, all of you," he said. "It will be all right in the morning."

Massingham got slowly to his feet.

"Amory," he began doubtfully; but the Parson's eyes were bright and his face transfigured.

"Hush, Massingham," he said. "Nothing you can say shall stop me. This is my duty, and I shall do it. I will crush this evil thing down into the everlasting fire of punishment—"

A quick cry broke in on him.

"Don't! Don't talk of everlasting punishment! You don't know what it means. God wouldn't – He *couldn't*–"

Amory smiled.

"Grindley, God is, before all, just. Evil must receive its reward. By God's grace, I hope to be His minister in dealing out that punishment."

Massingham looked at him heavily.

"Well – good luck," he said. Amory smiled, an odd smile of confidence, pity, and triumph. The door closed softly behind him.

For a few minutes there was silence. Then Grindley whispered:

"He can't *really* believe there's a God like that?"

No one answered; then Vernon, speaking for the first time that evening, muttered:

"Some evil deserves – anything."

He rose heavily and went out. A little later Grindley caught Reece's eye: the little curate laid down his book, and without a word the odd pair left the room together. Massingham and Ladislaw sat on and on in silence, Massingham smoking sombrely, Ladislaw nervously touching up the fire. At last the Scotsman dropped the poker with a clatter.

"Massingham," he said in a queer strained voice, "I can't bear this. What do you imagine is going on in there?"

Massingham stirred.

"God only knows!" he said. Then he added suddenly:

"I'm going to listen. Don't you come, Mac. I'd rather you didn't."

He went out, and Ladislaw heard his steps mounting the stairs, going along the corridor, fading into silence. In the smoking room the fire sank lower and the ashes fell softly.

In a few minutes Massingham returned, paler and looking a little apprehensive.

"Well?" asked Ladislaw.

"There's – something awful going on in there," said Massingham jerkily. "I don't know what. I heard Amory's voice – and hard breathing, and a kind of ghastly muffled moaning noise–"

Ladislaw sprang up.

"Moaning? Amory?"

Massingham shook his head.

"Amory's voice was steady enough," he said "It was like steel – ice – I don't know... He wasn't the – thing – that moaned."

Ladislaw shuddered.

"Could you hear what he said?"

"Not entirely," Said Masgingham reluctantly. He wiped his forehead, and Ladislaw saw that his hand shook.

The two men stared into each other's eyes.

"There was a smell like scorching," added Massingham suddenly, "and a horrible sound, like something cracking very slowly – or crushing, p'r'aps."

Again they stood in silence, straining their ears.

"Oh, for God's sake, let's go and stop it!" cried Ladislaw abruptly; and both men turned on an impulse and ran up the shallow wooden stairs.

At the top they came face to face with Amory himself. He stood staring blindly before him, his skin stretched and white over the bones of his face, his eyes wide and blank and horrified.

"Amory! Thank God you're here!" cried Massingham.

Amory stared on silently. Then suddenly he spoke.

"*The tears ran down over my hands,*" he said in an odd, strained voice. He held his hands, thin and dry and rigid, a little before him. Massingham and Ladislaw looked at them instinctively. Then Ladislaw touched Amory gently on the shoulder.

"Come away, man," he said in his soft Highland voice.

The lids blinked rapidly once over Amory's blank staring eyes. Otherwise he did not move. Ladislaw slipped his hand through the rigid arm. Together he and Massingham got Amory down the stairs.

The clock struck three as they passed through the hall, and the sound seemed to rouse Amory from his stupor of horror. He passed a hand rapidly over his face, and then looked in an odd bewildered way at the concerned faces of his two friends. He shuddered a little.

"Massingham—" he said in a troubled voice.

"Yes, Amory, all right, old chap," said Massingham.

"Massingham oh, Massingham, the tears ran down over my hands. I went on, and the tears ran down over my hands."

They sat with him till day came, a watery yellow rim between the wet earth and the weeping sky. They could hear the little sound as he passed his tongue over his dry lips.

The next day was Sunday. When Massingham's guests first came, there had been some talk of Amory's preaching in the village church to relieve the vicar, an old man in feeble health; but Massingham hardly liked to broach the subject to a man so utterly broken as Amory. But it seemed that he himself had not forgotten. He appeared at the breakfast-table, exhausted and livid, but composed; and at the end of the meal – through which he sat, silent and nervous, looking like a man who has passed through an agony – he spoke.

"What time is the service, Massingham?"

"Eleven. But, I say, Amory, you're not fit to preach."

"I know. I'm utterly unfit. But I must preach today, if I never enter a pulpit again."

"But, Amory, you're ill – done in. You ought to rest."

"*Rest!*" said Amory, raising his head for the first time; and at the look in his tortured eyes Massingham dropped his own.

It was an odd sermon, prefaced not by a single text, but by a reading from St. Paul's Epistle to the Corinthians – that famous passage that deals with charity. And Amory spoke in a voice strained to the point of quivering of the guilt of those who condemn their brothers. His usual beautiful style was gone. His sentences were harsh, abrupt, and broken. There was one strange passage, which he delivered as if under appalling physical stress, his white-knuckled hands clutching the pulpit, sweat beading his brow and lips.

"Years ago," he said, "men tried to convert their opponents by torture. They showed them the human version of hell. They ground their bones, scorched their flesh, tore their eyes." (Here he turned ashy white to the lips.) "The tears of their victims wetted their hands, and they lifted those hands, wet with tears and blood, to God, the merciful God, to ask His blessing and His help. We torture souls in the same Name. We condemn them to a lingering death of torture by despair. I have tortured a soul to death – crushed it, broken–"

He stopped, gasped audibly, opened his mouth once or twice, and then added abruptly, "Be merciful. You don't know – you can't judge other souls. Have mercy, always." He paused again, and then, in the astonished silence of the country church, abruptly left the pulpit.

That was the only reference he made to the appalling happenings of that night.

In the afternoon Ladislaw, Massingham and Vernon sat together at one end of the long library. Reece and Grindley, at the far end, talked together; Amory alone was absent.

"I say," said Massingham a little awkwardly, "don't you chaps think we've gone far enough? I mean, there's not much point in crocking ourselves over this confounded business, is there? Look at Reece, for instance; we don't want to push a simple-minded kid like that into this hell-hole. What do you think?"

"Reece won't hurt," said Vernon heavily.

"Oh, I don't know," said Massingham. "He's more sensitive than you'd think. Look what he's done for poor old Grindley. What do you say, Mac?"

"No one ought to go near that room," cried Ladislaw fiercely. "You're right, Massingham – hell-hole's the word for it."

Vernon opened his mouth and closed it without speaking.

"*I'm* not going!" said Ladislaw. "It's my turn tonight, isn't it? Well, I've got pluck enough not to go."

Vernon looked up at him with an odd questioning glance, and their eyes met.

"You know?" asked Vernon.

Ladislaw nodded. "Enough," he said. "I've seen things – at home. I know what might – anyway, I'm not going."

He rose and went towards the door; then he turned back.

"What about you, Massingham? Will you be wise in time and chuck it too?"

Massingham flushed a little.

"No, I don't think I'll chuck it," he said slowly. "Oh, I'm in a funk all right! But I can't exactly ask people here, and make them face – whatever's in that room – and not go myself, can I?"

Vernon suddenly broke in.

"Massingham – don't," he said, laying his hand on the other man's arm. "We, who've been – we'll understand. And Ladislaw will."

Massingham looked at him intently.

"I think I must go, Vernon," he said very quietly. "Besides, if Reece, why not me?"

Vernon got rather red.

"Look here," he said, "I've been, and I know what I'm talking about. Reece will be all right; but you – ! Don't ask why, Dick, but don't – don't go into that damned place."

Massingham looked gravely at Vernon's pleading face, and shook his head.

"I'm sorry, Bill," he said. Vernon stared with a kind of hopeless entreaty into his face, then turned away with a half-groan.

At eleven that night Massingham went to face his ordeal.

Massingham said nothing of his experiences when he joined his friends next day. Like those who had already met Fate in that room of his, he was very pale, and his eyes had that same piteous look – the look of one who has sinned past hope of forgiveness, and yet hopes, however faintly, that his friends may not cast him out. He spoke very little, and not at all of the subject that lay uppermost in all their minds. Only, when dusk was falling, and they all sat together in the long library, he said suddenly, breaking into the conversation with the manner of a man who has been totally abstracted:

"Reece, I want to ask something of you."

"Yes?" said Reece in his commonplace tone of cheerful willingness.

"Don't go into that ghastly room tonight."

The other voices had all died away, as does ordinary talk when the speakers hear the voice of a dying man. But Massingham's request was like the releasing of a spring – as if they had been waiting for a signal.

Amory spoke first,

"Reece, he's right," he said in a very gentle voice. "It's not necessary, and it's–" He gulped.

"Yes, Reece," chimed in Ladislaw, "don't go. Let me have a companion in my cowardice!" he added, with a half-laugh.

Grindley said nothing, but he looked at the little curate with a glance oddly compounded of confidence and entreaty, admiration and fear.

Reece looked at Vernon.

"What do you think, Vernon?" he asked.

Vernon hesitated: then:

"Go, if you like, I say," he said. "It's not as if you were – like the rest of us."

"*Vernon!*" broke in Massingham sharply. He knew that the two were utterly opposed, but really...! "Don't listen to him, Reece. Don't go. I tell you it's ghastly. No one can imagine it." He became very pale. "Don't go," he urged again.

Reece was still looking steadily into Vernon's eyes; neither wavered. Then the little curate turned to Massingham.

"I'm sorry, Massingham," he said, "but if you don't mind, I'd like to go. All the rest of you have been."

"Oh, if that's the way you look at it!" exclaimed Massingham bitterly. Then his voice dropped and sounded weary. "Have it your own way," he muttered. "I suppose it's your own look-out. You've been warned." He walked away.

The others glanced at each other. Was it of any use to say any more? Then they gave it up. After all, simple as he was, Reece was not a child.

Still, they all felt horribly uncomfortable when, shortly before eleven, Reece laid down the copy of *Punch* over which he had been chuckling for nearly an hour, and rose.

"Good-night, you chaps," he said. "See you in the morning."

Grindley half rose; Reece caught his eye and grinned.

" 'Night," he said again and, went out.

The others with one accord drew together round the fire. For a few minutes no one spoke.

"Good lord!" said Massingham suddenly. "I think this is the most horrible thing that's happened yet. He's such an utter kid to go into that pit of evil. He doesn't know – anything."

"If you come to that," said Amory, "I don't think any of us really knew what evil was. There's something in that room – God only knows what – some loathsome spirit of evil – that fills you until you become evil incarnate."

"There is – you're right!" cried Grindley excitedly. "You are – cut off. It's appalling–"

"It is appalling," said Massingham slowly, "to know that one is cut off oneself from hope of mercy or forgiveness. It is worse to cut off someone else."

They looked at him attentively.

"When one lets go the reins – allows blind fury to possess one utterly," said Massingham, still in that slow, almost detached voice, "one does not only kill one's own soul. There's the other soul. It's let out of the dead, heavy body – a damned soul, reproaching you for its damnation. And you can do nothing – nothing! It's – oh, I can't tell you! There aren't human words for a thing like that, which is inhuman."

The others remained silent.

"Have you ever thought," added Massingham abruptly, "how terrible it must be to be God? To know things like that, and let them be, because they're just?"

"God is merciful first and just afterwards," said Amory. "I know I used to say the reverse, but now I know better."

"You may be right," said Massingham. "There must be an amazing amount of goodness somewhere when there is such a quantity of unspeakable evil in men like us, who thought ourselves decent fellows enough."

Grindley moved impatiently.

"There is," he said; "I know there is. But I can't bear to think of that horror of evil, which we all know of, let loose on Reece. He knows all I could tell him, but you can't *tell* about–"

"No, you can't," agreed Amory.

"What I can't understand," said Massingham, "was why you were so – well, so callous – about it, Vernon. You had as ghastly a time as any of us, and yet, when you could have dissuaded that kid – (for you could have dissuaded him, only you could) – you let him go on."

"It's like this," said Vernon, and the others were astonished at the gentleness of his voice. "Since – that night – I've felt the most tremendous reverence for innocence – purity of mind and thought. It seems to me that evil can't touch it, but it might touch evil. Do you see what I mean? – You do, Amory."

"Y-Yes, I do," admitted the Parson; "but – oh, Vernon, it's the most ghastly risk! None of us ever guessed what would happen to the others, and we were more or less intimate with them. Now we know – (a little: we shall never know really) – what each has gone through; we can see how it worked. That room is so evil that when a man goes into it all the worst in him is drawn out. He is himself still, but filled and soaked with evil passions. He becomes vice incarnate–"

"Yes!" cried Vernon; "that's it!"

"What evil is in Reece?" asked Ladislaw.

They were silent a little, and then Grindley said apologetically: "You see, one knows him so little. As Amory said, we aren't intimate with him, any of us. We've only been in close contact with him just lately, when we're all abnormal. I don't know – I hate to think of him alone up there, unsuspecting–"

They fell silent again, like men who anxiously await news. Suddenly Ladislaw rose and went and opened the door. They all listened intently. The house was utterly still. Ladislaw came back, but he left the door open. "Just in case," he murmured, half-apologetically.

The night wore on. Somehow no one cared to go to bed. With the others it had been different – they could look after themselves; but they all felt a queer responsibility for Reece. He was such a kid, they kept saying, and the danger was so horrible. The dead silence of the house, dark and brooding beyond the open door of the warm and well-lit smoking-room, was terrible. Reece was out there, alone...

Dawn showed grey at last, and slowly the night lifted. The five men had been silent for the last hour or more. Now they looked dully, almost hopelessly, at each other's faces, grey in the early light, and silently they rose. It was over. Whatever had happened was ended.

They all felt a shock of surprise, relief – yes, and delight – when Reece came into the dining-room. He looked round at their drawn faces with concern.

"I say – is anything wrong?" he asked.

"No," said Massingham, with a half-laugh. "No; not if you're all right."

"Oh, *I'm* all right," said the little curate cheerfully. "Never slept better in my life, and that's saying a lot."

"Then, you saw—?" began Grindley.

"I didn't see a thing," said Reece half-regretfully. "Something missing in my make-up, I expect. It *is* a pity! However, I've had my chance."

And he fell hungrily on his breakfast.

THE CURE

IT WAS, I know my fault but though she never may – and I pray that she never will – realise it, it was even more Freda's. For it was Freda who implored me to undertake the whole thing saying in her brisk and decisive way "He must *vegetate*, Spud. It's his nerves. You understand. Let him just be quiet – do nothing and think nothing." And, again, "Make him into a *real vegetable* won't you?" Which shows, of course, that she knew nothing of Erik, though she was his twin. You could no more make a vegetable of Erik Storm than you could make a doorscraper of a violin. Though I didn't know that then. It's one of the things I learnt, down at Crows' Hall. And I learnt, too, that when it's the thoughts of a man that are distorted and flaming like a jungle it's the wickedest and silliest thing you can do to give his mind complete rest. Then, like a spider, his Idea (for everyone has an Idea that is the driving-power of his whole mind) begins to work and weave, out of its own substance, a filmy web that grows and tangles the mind until —

Well, you see how it is. I know these things now. I was, at the beginning of this story – if it is a story – the stolidest and stupidest of creatures. Which is exactly why Freda chose me as Erik's companion.

I'd grown up next door to the Storms, and we three – Erik and Freda and I – had played together. Erik invented the games out of his head – wonderful games, I daresay, for he was a wonderful boy; but Freda, who was quick and practical, and I, who was slow and literal, used to shriek with laughter sometimes over his wild fancies; and we could never see, as he could, all manner of beauties and terrors by "just thinking." So it generally ended in Erik's going off, sore and furious, to the bare sea-marshes, while Freda and I played the normal, ordinary games in the pretty secluded garden. When our games gave out – (two is a small number, and we were uninventive) – we used to go out and find Erik, sitting in the sea-lavender with his hands clasped round his knees, crooning to himself; or standing, silent, listening to the lonely wind creeping round the dunes. Most unhealthy. He'd generally forgotten all about the quarrel then. He never did remember his human relationships very well.

We didn't go to the same school. Erik went to some queer Scandinavian place – did I say that Mr. Storm was Scandinavian? Swedish or Norwegian or Danish, I forget which – and I went to a "lesser public school" near home. I was only a weekly boarder, and so I saw a lot of Freda still. She was a good pal – far more of a boy than a girl, though a good housewife even then. And I'm afraid we didn't miss Erik much. Then he went to Oxford; and I, who was far too stupid for a University, and had no desire whatever for one, took to farming in Sussex. Freda went on her brisk, interested way alone until she got married to a decent quiet chap called Martin. And then for some years I lost sight of the Storms – heard vaguely of Freda's babies – that Erik had gone abroad to Russia – that he was spending six months in Iceland – that he was doing research into Northern folklore. So *like* Erik, I thought.

Then, one day when I was in town on business, Freda and I ran into each other in Baker Street.

"Spud!" she said, rather breathlessly. "It's like a miracle. I believe I was praying to see you."

She slurred her r's, as she always did when she was excited.

"Were you?" I said stupidly. I hadn't seen her for over four years, but we always met like that – as though one of us had just been out of the room for a moment and had come back. "What's up?" I went on, for she looked quite disturbed.

"I can't tell you here," she said, looking round. "Can't we go somewhere and talk?"

"Madame Tussaud's—" I began. I was quite surprised when she began to laugh a little wildly.

"Spud! How like you!" she cried. "We meet after four years – you come like a miracle – and you propose to go to a waxwork show!"

"Not to see the waxworks," I explained patiently. I'd never seen Freda like that before. "To talk. It's quiet. It's generally empty at this time of year."

"I didn't even know there was really such a place... Well, let's go – anywhere to talk in peace – I *must* talk to you, Spud."

So we went. It was nearly empty – I knew it would be, in June – and we ordered tea in the place there. And Freda told me.

"It's Erik," she said, taking off her gloves very carefully. "He's – so funny, Spud."

I nodded. That was nothing unusual.

"He's... Well, you know how he went off into the North to find out sagas and charms and things? He found out a lot... and... I can't quite follow it all. He was alone, you know, alone there in the dark and the ice... He seemed – fascinated... He went about, farther and farther north. He opened tombs and things... and he found odd things, and heard – dreadful things... Spud, I think he got sort of – possessed. He used to go out alone at night to those awful old dead places... and he'd learned spells and charms and rites... And – and, Spud – I'm – afraid."

She broke off sharply. She was quite pale.

"He got ill. Of course he did, going out at night into that ghastly cold. I went to him. He was – I've never seen him like that before. He was frightened – oh, I can't tell you – *terrified*! He was delirious – he *shrieked* – and then he'd whisper, and whisper... Just scraps, but enough..."

Her voice was shaking so that she had to stop. After a little she went on more quietly.

"Well, I brought him home, back to the sun and warmth. His nerves are all to pieces. He's more or less controlled, now, but –

Well, honestly, Spud, I don't like having him in the house with the children. Peter's timid as it is, and he and Erik are always together. And then you came into my mind... I thought you might help... I don't know what to do."

I'd never seen Freda so distressed.

"Is he still ill – apart from nerves I mean?" I asked.

"Oh no – his *body's* all right. He needs to *vegetate* you know. He's been so worked up – so excited over all this silly magic business. And you're such a *calm* old thing Spud–"

It was then that she made the remark about my making a vegetable of Erik.

Well I needn't detail the whole thing. I went and saw – Freda ostensibly, but really the situation. Erik looked all right, I thought – pale and thin of course, but then he'd been ill; and his eyes looked odd. People's eyes often do, though, when their faces are thin. He was quiet enough, except that once, at dinner, he started up trembling all over and rushed into the garden. When he came back he muttered some silly rot about having heard a bat. Now one doesn't, you know, in Hampstead – or anywhere, as a rule, they squeak too high; I thought it a thin explanation... Oh yes, and he did get quite excited once when he noticed a queer old ring I was wearing. I always wear it since I turned it up one day when I was ploughing up on Wether Down – an ugly, heavy thing of some dull metal with queer shapes – runes, don't you call them? – cut on it. He got quite worked up – wanted the thing, and behaved like a spoilt child when I refused to part with it. I got quite annoyed – I am obstinate, I know. And Erik suddenly got up and went off somewhere alone, just as he used to when we were kids. Lord knows where he went to, though, in Hampstead...

Of course Freda had her way. I could see that Erik was nervy – Lord! what an inadequate word! But it really was all that I saw then – and Freda was naturally worried. And I am far too lazy to be anything but obliging. So, as I was going back to Sussex anyhow, I invited Erik. Freda and I thought that the farm would be just the place for him – so quiet, so uneventful, so calm... God! What fools sensible people are!

Now, I want to make two things quite clear. I never had, and didn't then, begin to understand Erik or anything about him. But I was tremendously sorry for him – he was so white and miserable and silent and (I know now) *haunted*. I wanted to do my best for him; only I didn't know what to do. I could only think of the silliest, most obvious attentions that one would pay to an invalid aunt.

I met him the night he came. I drove to the little station where there are three trains a day, because it seemed the thing to do. I remember it was a threatening looking night, and I hoped the rain wouldn't come just yet and beat down the hay. Erik was the only passenger, and he was absurdly glad to see me. I was quite moved.

"I was so afraid you wouldn't be here," he kept saying.

"Well, it wouldn't have been so far to walk if I hadn't come," I said once. "You could have left your stuff at the station."

He looked at me oddly and didn't answer.

"Besides, you'd probably have had company on the road," I went on.

He started then, and shivered violently. I remembered his illness, and told him to pull up the rug...

He seemed very listless at first – wouldn't even unpack properly, so my housekeeper, Mrs. Burns, told me. She is very tidy, and she seemed a bit annoyed. I can't risk that. So one evening I said to Erik:

"Got straight upstairs yet, Erik?"

"N-not yet," he said very slowly. "You see, I-I've brought a lot of stuff... unnecessary... curios, you know. I haven't sorted my things since I came south..."

He seemed quite confused about it.

"Well, would you like me to come up and give you a hand? Rather miserable, isn't it, having your collars and socks mixed up with coins and junk like that?"

He flushed scarlet.

"Oh, I-I don't – I'm afraid–"

I was extremely puzzled by his manner. Then he burst out:

"Well, if you really wouldn't mind coming *with* me–"

It sounded like a kid afraid of the dark! But I just thought that he was too tired after his illness to want to do anything on his own. I've never been ill, and I felt quite bright for thinking of it.

We went up to his room – and really I didn't blame Mrs. Burns. I'm not what you'd call neat myself, but this–! I'd never seen such a muddle. Bags and boxes and rucksacks all open and bulging with sweaters and shoes and books and all manner of things.

"You see, I wanted to find something – something I... not valuable, at all, but... I can't remember where I put things... I was ill, you know, and – *and I must find it*," he broke out.

He was awfully worked up.

"Well, let's put everything away," I said, "and we're bound to find it, if it's here. What is the thing, anyway?"

But he only muttered to himself, something in a language I didn't understand. I don't think it was the stuff he and Freda used to talk, though. It sounded more uncouth than that.

We'd nearly finished when he found the box. Quite an ordinary wooden box. He threw himself on it, like a kid with a toy. Then he began to open it, with a kind of rather horrible eagerness; and then – he suddenly began to tremble visibly, got deadly white, and hurled the thing to the other end of the room. It must have been fairly heavy, for it made quite a thud, and I thought I heard a chinking sound, like metal.

"Here! Don't go chucking treasure trove about like that!" I said, making a desperate effort to be jocular because I was too bewildered to do anything else.

I went across to pick the thing up, but Erik jumped at me and clutched my arm.

"Don't *touch* it, don't *touch* it," he kept gabbling in a queer hoarse whisper. "Come away – do come away..."

I was afraid he was going to be ill again. He looked like death.

Now, as I say, I hadn't the faintest idea what the chap was after or what to do; but I was simply aching with pity. So I thought I'd better just do what he wanted – humour him, you know. We went downstairs together. He clung on to my arm all the way, and, though his hands shook and trembled, there were bruises there when I went to bed.

Well, I'm not what's called imaginative, Lord knows! But it was a queer business, wasn't it? and Erik – I simply can't begin to tell you what he looked like with his white face and staring black holes of eyes, and his terror – for it was nothing else. I'd never in my life – then – been afraid; not of the dark when I was a kid nor of animals nor accidents nor people nor, I'm afraid, God or the Devil. I suppose it was because I had no imagination. But that night I felt – well, uncomfortable, no more – for the first time in my life.

The sight of my cheery room with its wood fire and the bright warm light and the curtains and sporting prints put me right before I knew I was wrong. It was a ripping room, that. Pity I shall never see it again...

Even Erik seemed better in there. We sat down, one on each side of the fire (it was a chilly night, I remember, for June) and I, to give him time to recover himself, messed about with my pipe, which didn't need any attention whatever. Again I rather patted myself on the back for my tact in this. But there was no betting on Erik.

"For heaven's sake stop scraping that pipe, Spud," he cried quite suddenly. "It doesn't want it, and – and I can't bear it..."

I'm afraid I gaped. He was beyond me. I'd no idea anyone could mind a little noise like that.

He smiled at me suddenly, like a kid.

"Oh, Spud, I'm sorry! I am an ungrateful brute," he said. He was the most disarming chap.

"Bosh, old thing," I said. "Only, you see I'm such a tough sort of bear. You'll have to tell me every time I get on your nerves, because I simply don't know enough to keep off."

He smiled again. Now I've never seen any eyes in the least like Erik's. They could be so bright and blue that they quite startled you and then in a second they'd be dead black – not what you generally call black but real black, all over. Extraordinary they were. And you could generally tell his mood by the colour of his eyes. Now they were as blue as the sea is on an August afternoon when you look over from Wether Down.

"Spud, you're a – I mean, I'm most tremendously glad you're

here," he said. "I want – I say, may I tell you something – something about what happened–"

I quite forgot Freda and the cure.

"I wish you would," I said.

"I don't know if you'll ever understand," said Erik slowly. "It'll sound the most putrid rot, I expect. Perhaps it is! Anyhow, I can't tell whether it is or not until I say it out to somebody else. If you go on turning a thing over in your own head you can get to believe *anything*."

Now I know that he was right. You can. But then I said,

"Rot! Either a thing's true or it isn't. No amount of thinking will make truth into a lie or a lie into truth."

He smiled again, rather sadly.

"Well – I don't know," he said. "Anyhow, I want to tell you."

So he began telling me how he'd gone to Norway and Iceland and these other places to do research into a dead life. Folklore and charms and dead religions and legends and things. He found out quite a lot, apparently: anyhow he got absolutely fascinated.

"I can't tell you how it gripped me," he said. "It was – extraordinary stuff. And the more I looked the more I found. I simply can't tell you... I went north, and I met a man – old – oh, incredibly old. And he showed me how to see and to hear... One night, after he knew me a bit, we went to a barrow..."

His breath seemed to stop completely. He was quite white, like paper, and his eyes seemed to have gone into his head. They were black and dead.

I couldn't understand in the very least. What was there to alarm or disturb the chap? He didn't say what he'd seen and heard, of course, but still–!

"My dear Erik," I said, "what a kid you are! You get an old Swede or Dane or something to tell you ghost stories, and you go out at night with him to some old tomb thing – and you're upset for months! What did you do at the barrow?"

He shuddered violently. He tried to say something, but his voice died before I could hear it.

"What does one do at a barrow?" I went on jocularly: "You bury old kings and warriors, don't you, with jewels and cups and things, in chambers inside a burial mound? Did you look for any loot?"

He nodded; and suddenly I saw light. "What – the box upstairs? You pinched some treasure? Oh, Erik, you *priceless* old fool!" I was weak with laughing. "I'm going to have a look."

I ran upstairs whistling and went into Erik's room. There lay the box where he'd pitched it. I went towards it, when something rushed past me, snatched it up, and hurled it right through the window.

It was Erik. He turned on me, eyes blazing, chest heaving – looked as if I'd tried to murder him!

"My dear chap!" I said when I could speak. "I wasn't going to hurt the thing. What the devil's the matter? – Don't stare at me like that!" I snapped. "You've lost the bally thing now, not me. And you've broken a window into the bargain."

His face changed. He got a bit more colour and his eyes looked saner. He looked like a man waking out of a dream, bewildered and a little ashamed.

"I – I'm awfully sorry," he muttered. "I don't know – I can't explain. Let's go downstairs. I'm awfully sorry," he repeated.

When we were back before the fire I tried to get him to tell me what had happened at the barrow and what was in the box and why he'd got so mad: but he would say not one word. I'd shut him up for good. Only, just as we were going up to bed, he turned to me at the door in his old frank way.

"Spud," he said, "look here. I'm no end sorry about this. It shan't happen again. I'm going to chuck all this stuff – these dead things. I'm going to be sane – *if I can*. You'll help me, won't you, not to go back to them?"

"Why the devil should you ever go near Iceland again if you don't want to?" I said. He puzzled me hopelessly.

"I don't necessarily mean Iceland... Oh, I can't explain! I hate it, and I long for it – I loathe it, and I must have it! It's like a drunkard... Spud, keep me away from it!"

It was like a frightened kid asking you to keep ghosts off. All I could say was, "It'll be quite all right, old chap. This isn't Iceland, you know. No icefields and barrows here. Only good farmed land and friendly country... Now let's get to bed."

"It isn't only Iceland," he said slowly. "It's everywhere – if you look... But I won't look. I'll chuck it. I *will*."

And for some days after that he was quite normal and cheerful – seemed quite interested in the farm and the beasts and labourers and so on. Asked a lot about the history of the place, I remember, and why the valley behind Wether Down, where the mounds are, was called Kings Bottom... He spent the day fooling round, picking up stories from the countryfolk and getting to know the lie of the land. I only saw him at meals, and then he was so contented and happy that I cheered loudly and wrote to tell Freda that our cure was working and that Erik had quite forgotten his old dead ghosts and gods.

It was, perhaps, a week after that that I had to ride over to Marden le Winken, which is a village about a mile from the farm. It's the sort of little place that I like because it has a small life of its own, and – oh, well, it's homely. Artists come there and gas about the green and the old well and the church, until in sheer self-defence I retort with plain speaking about sanitation, which generally makes them sheer off. Well, that day – a very clear, hot, July day with a cloudless sky that looked as if it never could change or darken – I pulled up on the green; and there, sitting on the well coping I saw Erik and another person, I couldn't quite make out whom. They were staring down the well as if they'd lost something. Now I'm always a bit anxious when nervy people start gazing earnestly at water or down cliffs or anything like that; so I called out to Erik.

"Oi! Erik!" I shouted. "Come here half a tick, will you?"

He got up and came over, walking as if he were in a trance. And then I got a start. Erik, of course, was queer and one made allowances, but his companion was Murky Glam the village idiot!

Now I'm not an absolute brute and I've a kind of respect for "God's children" as Sussex people still call imbeciles. But I don't like them. I don't like anything deformed or abnormal. Still, I'd often spoken to Murky Glam – (no one knew why he was called that or what his real name was) – and he'd sometimes been over to Crows'

Hall with a message or something; and often and often, when I've been ploughing up on the downs above Kings Bottom, I've come across Murky sitting there on one of the humps that stand above the valley where the ancient yew-trees grow. But it's one thing to speak civilly to a chap when you meet him, and quite another to sit with him for hours looking down a well. And I didn't think that a village idiot was a very good companion for Erik anyway.

Well, it was a blazing hot day, and I'd been annoyed at having to leave the farm, and I'd been delayed by a man on the way in, and then Erik had startled and almost frightened me; so I snapped at him.

"What the devil were you doing at that well?" I asked.

Erik looked straight through me as if I wasn't there. I don't believe he knew who I was. He said nothing at all.

"*Erik!*" I said angrily.

He seemed to wake up.

"Oh! Did anyone – did you speak to me?" He asked in the queer half-foreign accent he always had when he was dreaming.

"Yes," I snapped, "I did. I should think you could have heard me half a mile away. What the deuce are you doing with that chap?" And I jerked my head towards Murky Glam.

Erik looked at me and I felt like a blustering bully.

"I was talking," he said very quietly.

"You weren't," I said bluntly.

He flushed scarlet and turned away.

"Erik!" I said, "hold on. I'm sorry. I didn't mean to be rude. But you know–"

He didn't seem to be listening. He was walking very slowly back to the well. Murky Glam took no notice whatever of either of us. It really was a bit uncanny. Broad midday – glorious summer weather – the homely little village green – and that chap dressed in rags, with odd bright patches and a broken cock's feather stuck in his hat, sitting staring at the well. The water, like a bright eye twinkling in the sun, seemed to stare back. And there was Erik – my vegetating charge – walking straight into this fantastic picture.

I can't tell you why, but I felt quite alarmed. It was like seeing a child walk over the edge of a cliff.

I vaulted down and caught Erik up.

"Erik!" I said, laying hold of his arm. "Erik – you *said* you'd chuck it."

I didn't myself know what he was to chuck.

He stood quite still; slowly he turned and faced me. Then he looked back at the well. Murky Glam was sitting up now, and looking at us with an idiot's silly smile.

"You promised," I said again.

"Yes. I know I did," muttered Erik, his eyes on Murky Glam. "I will – I *will*."

And he turned and went slowly off down the road to Crows' Hall. He'd made quite a sensation in the village – of course he had! – and I knew there'd be endless chatter, which I hate. I was awfully annoyed. I made the best of it by turning into the inn, and casually mentioning that Erik was interested in imbeciles – I'm afraid I purposely gave the impression that he was a doctor on a holiday – and then I went on to the woman who calls herself Murky Glam's mother and told her that I wouldn't have the chap coming down to Crows' Hall. It would have been about as useful to tell the fire not to let the kettle boil...

I was, even for a working farmer, quite exceptionally busy just then. The harvest was coming on in that sudden rush that sometimes happens when a hot August follows a wet July. There were storms knocking about, too, and I wanted to harvest as soon as possible. Then Bates, my excellent cowman, slipped on a greasy stone floor and broke his leg, and, as I didn't trust his boy, I had to do most of the cow work myself. I'm not trying to make excuses. I know now that I ought to have lost the crops and even let the cows suffer rather than have allowed what happened. And I ought to have had my eyes opened, too, after that hot blue morning in Marden le Winkin. But on a farm you lose sight of everything but the land and the beasts. I thought myself lucky if I got off with a seventeen-hour day, and I rolled into bed only to sleep like a log. Even at meals I was preoccupied with plans and details of farm work, and only noticed that Erik was very quiet, and often late for meals. Sometimes I hardly saw him all day, for he cut out his food altogether as far as we could see, and only said he'd been "out" when I questioned him.

It was Gibson, my head carter, who finally put me on to the track. We were making the arrangements for the great harvest supper that is always held at Crows' Hall, whoever the owner, on August 15th – Lammas Night. It's the event of the year there. There's a big meal first, with lots of beer and cider, and afterwards there's a "bale-fire" on the biggest mound in Kings Bottom. We had just finished our plans when Gibson made his remark.

"Mr. Storm seems rare taken up wi' they mounds over to Kings Bottom," he said. "Always down among 'em he is, along o' that wastrel Murky Glam."

I jumped, I don't deny it.

"Murky Glam?" I said. "I warned him off my land days ago."

"Big mound ain't Crows' Hall prop'ty, not by rights it ain't," said Gibson. "You stops at second mound sir, if all was as it should be."

"Then how can I have the bale fire on the big mound, you fool?" I cried. I was annoyed for we'd spent valuable minutes in discussing that very fire and Gibson had seemed to take the site for granted.

"That'll be all right, sir," answered Gibson placidly. Good chap, he knew what a time I'd been having, and he made allowances for me, though he did have that maddening air that country people so often have of kindly pity for the poor idiot who doesn't know their customs. "Lammas Fire's always been on that mound, long's any on us can mind. That's the place for 'im. But if you'll allow *me*, sir," (a favourite phrase of Gibson's, that) "you'll take care on 'en this year. See, it's the seventh year."

"*What's* the seventh year?" I asked, bewildered and a bit exasperated.

"It's like this, sir. Bale-fire, he always goes up on big mound, like I was a-tellin'. Only, once in seven years, summat happens, like. Old folks they say it's the toll taken by *him*." He jerked his thumb up at the mound. He was desperately solemn. "Seven year ago it were Ben Puckey – nice serious chap as you'd wish to see, Ben were, and booklearned along wi' it. Left supper early, he did, an' never went 'ome. Nex' day he weren't at work. 'I'll tell 'ee where to find 'en,' says old gaifer Gregory. 'Look in ashes up on big mound,' he says. An' true, there he were... Poor Ben, a nice young chap as you'd meet. Seven year afore that it were young Mr. Jerrold from Combes – young chap up at Oxford College. Not so much loss he weren't. Afore that it were old Gaffer Tomlyn and afore that–"

"*Gibson!* Don't be an ass!" I shouted. "Do you want me to believe that someone's bound to die on the mound every seventh year?"

"'Tain't what I asts you to believe," said Gibson with dignity. "It's truth, take it what way you like."

I thought a minute. One has to be rather careful, even with the most sensible men, over their pet beliefs; and I'd certainly heard something about young Jerrold – yes, and about Ben Puckey too...

"Gibson, look here," I said. "I don't deny that there have been deaths there. I'm not a fool, and facts are facts. But don't you think it's just because people expected them? They think there'll be one – and so of course there is. Look at these men you've mentioned. Gaffer Tomlyn was 'toteling,' wasn't he? Over ninety, I've heard. He'd got it on his mind that there must be a death there that year. Young Mr. Jerrold – well, you all know he was in with a wild set – drink and Hellfire Club and devil-worship and the rest. And poor Ben had books and legends and charms on the brain. They were all ripe for it. So when the seventh year came, they – they just–"

"Quite so, sir," said Gibson in his politest and most chilling manner, which he always put on when he didn't in the very least agree with me and meant to stick to his own way. "All I say is, sir – best be careful come Lammas. It's been like that long's I can mind."

That was so like the Crows' Hall men. "Been so as long as we can mind" – and therefore always must be so! The job I had to get them to take to new methods and machinery you simply wouldn't believe... I just shrugged my shoulders.

"Oh! all right," I said; and made a private resolution to talk to Erik.

I didn't forget to; but it wasn't so easy to get the chance. I hardly ever saw him, and when I did he – how can I put it? – he didn't seem to know I was there. It was as if we lived in different worlds.

Sitting at the same table, or beside the same hearth, we were like beings of two different creations, unable to understand or speak or even see each other. Like disembodied spirits in different spheres – or a man and a spirit. I expect that's nearer the truth...

August 15th was a blazing day. I remember thinking there must be thunder about behind the fierce purplish sky, and my joy as I thought that, after this one field, all the crops would be in. The men worked like Trojans, for I'd said that three of them could go to prepare the fire if the others made up for their absence. We slaved and sweated in that field, and, as I write, I can smell the dry scent of the ripe wheat and the baked earth, and see the tiny flowers, speedwell and pimpernel, that we trod underfoot... The sea, five miles away over Wether Down, shimmered in a haze. The new rick looked silvery white against the deep intensity of the sky.

I hadn't time to eat or speak or think that day. Apart from the ordinary work, there was the big barn to prepare for the harvest supper, the carving to do, the beer and cider to tap, the fire to prepare. I worked like a man possessed. I forgot everything but the jobs that seemed to press in on me in an endless and urgent succession. I only remember one extraneous thought – and that was that I wished Erik would help a little. Looking back now, that thought seems to me the grimmest comment possible on that night.

The supper was, I believe, a great success. I know I carved and poured and poured and carved for what seemed like hours, and the men ate and drank enormously, and finally cheered and cheered. Then we went out to Kings Bottom.

The moon was up by then – a great pearl, floating in a kind of insolent calm over the rolling fields. It was miraculously clear. Every blade of stubble, every stone, every leaf, seemed etched in the flood of light. The sky was huge and empty and only a moonlit sky is empty. Oddly enough, for me, a line of poetry slid into my mind—

"The moon doth with delight look round her when the heavens are bare."

The country was like an incarnation of that line. And then, quite suddenly, with a rush and a roar of flame, the bale-fire sprang into life.

It was magnificent. In that remote valley under the quiet darkening sky, the huge fire leaped and towered upon the tomb of a long-dead king; and the men stood round it, grave, patient, like the soil itself. I seemed to have a sudden glimpse of some truth I'd always known and never understood – some truth about men and the earth and the kinship of things...

Then someone began a song, and there was a certain amount of skylarking, and people went through old, half-forgotten rites and charms; and the quiet moon sailed higher in the darkling sky, as if contemptuous of our antics.

I was suddenly very tired. The fire was sinking and the fun was over. I thought of bed, and decided that I needn't wait. I rather wished Erik had been there – he'd have been interested in the charms and things – and then I thought, impatiently, God forgive me! what a hopeless chap he was to have to do with, and that if he preferred to fool round with an idiot he could – I couldn't dry-nurse him, in addition to all my other tasks. I decided to clear out. After all, I'd done my job. They'd had their feed and their fire, and the crops were in, and Gibson's gloomy croakings about the seventh year were disproved, and all was well. So I said goodnight, and went back to Crows' Hall.

Yes, all was well, I thought again, going down through the reaped fields, and the rickyard with the big firm solid stacks, and the quiet farmyard where the horses moved a little, heavily, in their stalls, and the young calves rustled in their litter. Thunder might come, and rain and hail; but for me at least all was well.

I fell asleep at once. It was the heavy, dreamless sleep that you get after hours of heavy outdoor work and a good bit of anxiety that ends in peace. It must have been some hours later when I woke and saw the light on my wall.

My first thought was of lightning; then I knew it was fire, and thought of the rickyard. Then, at the window, I saw it, streaming up from the King's Mound – a column of fire, steady as a pillar, vivid under the night sky, the quiet empty fields spreading round it.

At first I saw no one; then, quite unmistakably, even at that distance, I saw the weird figure of Murky Glam.

He moved slowly round the solitary fire, making odd fantastic gestures which were yet solemn, and to me, horribly impressive. And then, quite suddenly, I saw something in the midst of the flame.

I think I knew even then what it was. I tore out of the house like a man possessed. I don't think anyone has ever run as I ran that night, barefoot and terrified, to the big mound that overlooks the sea lying like the rim of a silver shield beyond it. I ran blindly, in a red mist that seemed to me to be the light of the bale-fire: my ears roared, and I thought it was the flames, and ran on. I could taste the salt of my own sweat as it ran into my mouth; the breath tore roughly at my heart and throat. And even as I ran I knew I was too late...

The fire had sunk when I got there. A few little flames flickered timidly in the ashes, and licked at the hands of the man on the mound.

Murky Glam had vanished. Erik lay quite alone, his face turned up to the moon, his mouth smiling. His hands, lying on his breast, were folded about a little pile of ashes, where lay lumps of shapeless metal. Only his hands were singed badly. Above them a knife haft protruded from his bare breast. On the tomb the sacrifice had been offered; and the eternal moon looked down on the quiet and fruitful earth.

THE TREE

AFTERWARDS, when it was too late, people said they ought never to have married. It is always a risk, said the wiseacres, for two artists; and when one of them is a wild untamed genius like young Carstairs, well, it's madness, pure madness, and Nan deserved all she got... And then, thinking of Nan's face, so white against her black bobbed hair, and the tragic blue stare of her wide eyes, they would sometimes wish they hadn't said that.

The studio wasn't in, or even near, Chelsea. For one thing, Chelsea was dear; for another, it was obvious; for a third, it was crowded. So finally Carstairs, who knew every byway of London as a shepherd knows each nook on the moors where he spends his quiet days, found the place, in an odd little paved court near the old Law Courts.

It was a long, low room that had been used as a store, a gymnasium, a Church Room, a Socialist Club, a dance-hall and heaven only knows what as well. It had a sort of dignity from its very usefulness; its proportions were good – honest lines that gave it even a sort of beauty. Inside, its length was not as great as appeared from without, because two rooms had been cut off – one a tiny cupboard that Nan said she could use as a kitchen, and one big enough for a bedroom. The rest was the studio, and Carstairs had extra windows put in to get the right light.

It was very quiet, that long, low studio. Its big, clear windows looked out on to a little paved court surrounded by a wall of old brick. Pale tender grass sprouted up between the paving stones: and in the middle of the little yard there was a huge spreading ash tree. It was the tree that made Nan long for the place.

"It'll be like a picnic," she said, "living in a barn, with the tree overhead like an extra roof."

"I don't like the tree," said Ralph Carstairs, with that stubborn air he sometimes had that made him look like a nice sturdy boy of about ten. "It's too close," he added; and Nan suddenly had an odd fancy that he looked afraid, like a small boy who won't own that he is scared.

Not that the tree darkened the studio. Far from it; it filled the place with a green, quivering light that made you think of "sandstrewn caverns cool and deep, where the winds are all asleep." It was romantic, mysterious. It had the same effect of magic and gnomes that you feel in deep, damp woodland dells in the height of a hot summer. But Carstairs didn't feel it like that. He didn't like it.

"It's too close," he repeated, and explained that he meant "near" not the other kind of close. It was – intrusive, he said, feeling for the right word; predominant – looming too large. And Nan, who was quite extraordinarily sweet and unselfish, in spite of her twenty-two years and her freelance journalist's life, agreed with a sigh that it must come down if Ralph felt like that about it. Because he was going to be great and nothing must interfere with his work.

So Carstairs wrote to the landlord and the day was fixed for the execution – for somehow you felt it like that, the tree had such a personality – it was, as Ralph said, so dominant.

The men came to prepare it on the evening before they were to cut it down. It was April, and a lovely evening of misty gold, the sort of evening that makes you think of budding woods and primroses starry in deep hedges and birds building and fluting to one another. Carstairs was tired. He had been painting all day, and the spring was in his blood like a madness. He went to the windows for the felling of the tree; and then he turned back into the studio with a sigh of mingled relief and regret. For trees in April have a kind of claim, and the ash tree reared itself so magnificently against the pale clear sky, where already a faint star gleamed.

Nan was in her cupboard-kitchen cooking supper in a saucepan over a gas ring. When she came in to lay the table, Ralph was lying on the couch, asleep. He looked so infinitely tired that she decided not to disturb him, and sat down to wait till he should wake.

He was dreaming. Not dreaming happily, with the bliss of deep repose after a long spell of work, but restlessly, turning his head from side to side and muttering a little. Soon she could even hear what he said.

"*One – two – three,*" he whispered. "Listen to them – heavy – heavy – striking at it... How strong it is! Will it *never* fall? *Oh, I can't bear it!*" he suddenly cried out, starting up on the couch. "Stop, stop! Don't strike again! I can't bear–"

Nan went over, soothing him as if he had been a child.

"Darling, it's all right," she crooned. "It's not hurt. They haven't touched it yet. It's all right, Ralph."

He turned on her bewildered eyes, dazed with dreams.

"I thought – they were cutting down the tree," he muttered. "It's horrible – murderous. It – it hurt me – they were striking at me too..." He paused, puzzled. Already the vividness of the dream impression was fading. "They struck and struck at it... It wouldn't fall..." he said. Then, urgently, "It's still there Nan, isn't it?"

"Yes, sweetheart," she answered quietly. Her heart ached for him though she couldn't understand his anguish; his rumpled hair and bewildered eyes made him look so like a small boy.

He looked out of the window. The great branches spread and soared against the pale sky. The lines of the ropes placed by the workmen clung to it like the monstrous tentacles of some vile reptile seeking to sap its mighty strength.

"Nan – they mustn't go on. It – I must stop it. Nan, do you understand? I – it's – I must stop it."

"All right, old thing," said Nan tranquilly. "Go round now and tell them not to do it. Give them something for their trouble. I'll have supper ready when you get back."

And so the tree was spared; and Nan, who had always loved it with a warmth she could hardly explain even to herself, could have sung with glee.

All that spring she rejoiced, whenever she looked at it. It wasn't till she saw Ralph's big picture that she began to regret.

She knew the idea of the picture. It was to be called "Dawn." It was a dim, half-light picture of a stretch of rough heathery ground, barred by a wet, rutty track gleaming in the silver light of a cold dawn. There was in the picture a physical feeling of wet, chill, pure air – you could feel it on your face. And it was spacious and vast, so that you got an impression of the unity of earth and sky, and the feeling of that pause that seems to come into the life of things just at the dawn... And when Nan looked at it, late in May, Ralph had painted into it the ash tree. It loomed up in the foreground, malignant as ash trees are malignant: and the meaning of the picture – its purity and cold truth – were lost in romantic suggestion.

"Oh, Ralph!" cried Nan. "I *don't* like the tree."

Ralph looked at her oddly and said nothing.

"*Why* did you put it in?" she wailed. "It's wicked – witchcrafty – and your picture was so cold and pure and quiet–"

He laughed, a hard, almost cruel little laugh.

"Good for you, Nan," he said, almost with a sneer. "Didn't you know that ash trees were the special property of witches?"

"I-I don't know... But *why* have you put it in, Ralph? It – it's spoiling it. Can't you paint it out – get rid of it? *Do.*"

He looked at her, and she felt quite suddenly and unreasoningly afraid.

"I can't get rid of it now," he said slowly. "I missed my chance. I shall never get rid of it now."

"I don't mean the real tree," cried Nan, rather pale.

"What is 'real?'" he asked sombrely; and she was silent.

The picture was rejected. A man who was on the selection committee, and who had known Nan in her bachelor days, told her in confidence that it was the fault of the tree.

"It's in the wrong key," he said. "It spoils the atmosphere."

Those words haunted her. "It spoils the atmosphere," she thought, moving about the green-shadowed studio. "It spoils the atmosphere," she thought as she lay in bed and watched its royal branches stirring a little against the quiet sky. She grew to hate the tree.

That was a very trying summer; Nan herself was unusually irritable and depressed, and she thought that perhaps the difference she felt in Ralph was as much her fault as his – at least, she tried to think so. She was busy with her journalistic work, and when she saw how things were going she wisely kept out of Ralph's way as much as she could. There was no use, she told herself, in getting on each other's nerves more than was necessary. But she had an odd feeling of being out of it whenever she returned to the studio; she just didn't belong...

She must, I think, have guessed a little; but it was not until July that she knew for certain. One afternoon towards the end of the month she came in to find Ralph holding a kind of review of all his work for the past weeks – ever since March, in fact. There were a good many paintings – and the ash tree was in them all.

It dominated Ralph's work as it dominated the studio – yes, as, she now knew, it dominated Ralph himself. Great, uncanny, suggestive and beautiful, it reigned in them all. Even in the portrait of Sir Evan Penrith, that commission that had meant such a feather in Ralph's cap, the tree reared itself above the crude, hasty portrait, threatening and insistent. It was in the work like a subtle poison.

Nan felt suddenly and terribly afraid. She said nothing; but she looked up at the great tree, dark against the blazing blue of the sky, and she felt certain that it knew... This was vengeance, she thought; and she felt terribly impotent and small and desolate.

She said not a word about the pictures; and Ralph never seemed to notice her silence. His eyes were fixed on the tree, as if he expected – something; Nan didn't give it a name.

Nan was plucky, but she was not the stuff of which criminals are made. She was not sufficiently ruthless. It needed a great, almost an incredible, effort for her to decide on the step she took. But of one thing she was sure – that tree was becoming part of Ralph. It was obsessing him – his thoughts, his work, his very being. And she believed that only by the death of the tree could she free him from its mastery. She could not have it cut down – Ralph would prevent that. But there are other ways of killing a tree...

How she first heard of it I have no idea. I know that she had dealings with an old Sussex man she'd come up against in Limehouse in her journalist life – a man who had been a "diviner" and knew strange secrets of the earth; and I know it was from him that she got the stuff she used. But I know no more than that, and I can't ask her. Anyhow, her courage and her love helping her, she did it. She poisoned the ash tree.

That was a very sultry August, full of storms that never broke, with an air like grey wool and a sky livid with heat. Nan is imaginative, artistic, highly-strung... I don't know. Perhaps she is mistaken... But I don't believe she is.

Once, in the height of her distress, she said a few words that gave a clue. She had cut the bark, she said, slipping out at night under the moon to do it; she smeared the stuff in the wound she made. She hated doing it, she said, with a little shuddering gasp, *hated* it. It was treacherous, loathsome... But it was the tree or Ralph, and that of course meant that she had no choice... And she told herself that, every time she made another little wound and rubbed the poison stealthily in.

At first she felt almost happy. Her heart was at ease because she had taken the great step. She was saving Ralph, she thought, and that upheld her when her heart smote her for the murdered tree, already drooping a little in its topmost branches and sicklied in the rich green of its leaves. The studio was gaspingly hot, and she always felt restless in there because of the doomed tree drooping at the window; and so she took to avoiding the place – slipping out by herself, telling herself that she was glad, glad because she was saving Ralph.

When Ralph first began to flag, she thought it was the heat.

"If only it would thunder," she used to murmur wistfully, watching him as he sat idle, silent and brooding, his head drooping forward, his eyes fixed vacantly.

But the thunder hung in the air, or only growled sullenly far off; and the air lay on your lungs like a poultice, hot and clammy.

One day Ralph suddenly spoke.

"Nan," he said, "what's the matter with the ash tree?"

There was something like mockery in his listless voice as he spoke.

Nan glanced up, startled and guilty: but he was not looking at her. He was staring out at the tree.

It was drooping now in all its branches. Its pale leaves hung like dead things in the languid air. In every line it spoke of decay and death.

"I expect – the heat," murmured Nan.

"Yes. The heat. And that's what you think is wrong with me, too... Yes, you're right. The same with us both... Of course it is – You know, Nan," he said, suddenly facing round and looking at her with an odd, wild smile, "we're connected, that tree and I. You knew that, of course. You've felt it. That's why I couldn't kill it. It meant killing myself..."

Nan's heart stopped beating. She stared at him in wild alarm and horror. For she suddenly knew that it was the truth. And now it was too late. The poison had done its work...

AT SIMMEL ACRES FARM

I MUST explain first that I didn't know Markham very well. We lived on the same stair at Comyn (I don't think I'll give the real name of our college), but he was one of those large, vigorous people who live for Rugger and rowing, and I am no good at games on account of my short sight. I want to lay some stress on my sight, because it may account for other things. I don't believe it does, but it may. I hope it may.

It happened late in the Hilary term of our second year that Markham got rather badly damaged in a Rugger match. It was some injury to the back, not very serious, but it meant that he had to lie up for some weeks; and as we were of the same year and on the same stair, it also happened that I used to go in and see him a good deal; so when he asked me to come down to the Cotswolds with him for part of the vac. I rather jumped at it. I haven't many friends of my own – I am dull and priggish – and I expect he didn't want any of his own hefty pals about while he was so badly out of it. So, odd as we were as a pair, we fitted in rather well.

He chose the place – said his family used to come from those parts, and he had a liking for the country. It was a farmhouse, standing alone in wide, prosperous fields. We went there by car, on account of Markham's back, and I shall never, even now, look back on that evening with anything but pleasure. It was the twentieth of March, I remember, and there was a kind of green bloom on the bare fields and a purple bloom on the bare woods that lay on the hill behind the farm. The house itself was like a dozen others in that country – long and low, built of the yellow Cotswold stone, with a beautifully pitched roof and mullioned windows. The stone barns grouped about it showed the same beauty of perfect proportion. The whole thing was as simple and direct as the country it stood in.

I said something of this to Markham, but he hardly answered. He seemed fidgetty and uneasy; I thought he was probably in pain, or overtired with the journey. Anyhow, he only growled, rather shortly, that it was all rot, one farm was like another, and he hoped they'd give us decent meals. But he threw a queer, almost suspicious glance round as he was being helped in. I dismissed it as of no importance.

In the morning he was more cheerful. It was a lovely day, soft as April, with a tender blue sky that showed up the bursting leaf-buds. It was not a day to be in, ill or well; so I consulted Mrs Stokes as to the possibility of getting Markham out.

She had a sofa long and broad enough for him, and was perfectly willing that I should take it out; but when I asked her about a suitable spot to establish him in she rather hesitated.

"Haven't you a small garden or a patch of grass somewhere near the house?" I asked.

She looked quite troubled and confused.

"Well, of course," she said at last, "there's the plot in there," and she jerked her head at a high stone wall with a wooden door in it at one end of the yard; "but I don't think your friend would like it, sir," she added hurriedly. "Nobody's been there for years, and it's likely all choked wi' nettles and rubbish."

I was surprised to hear this. The farm was so well-ordered and the fields so clean that it seemed odd that a piece of ground so near the dwelling-house should be neglected.

"May I look at it?" I asked: and again I couldn't help seeing that she went for the key of the door with considerable reluctance.

While she was gone I studied the outside of this yard. It ran on to one end of the farmhouse, as if it had once been the flower-garden of some bygone farmer's wife; but instead of coming right up to the house wall, a high wall of its own cut it off from the house. This seemed absurd and ridiculously inconvenient since, of course, it meant that the rooms on that side of the house could have no windows, whereas they might have looked out pleasantly on to a garden. The high wall ran round three sides of the little plot and at the fourth end, opposite the house, I could see the pointed end of a stone barn.

I'm sorry if I'm tedious, but I must explain this still more. This fourth wall was apparently the end of a ruined barn which had at one time, before the garden was made, run straight on to the house. You could tell this because a bit of the roof remained, projecting over the plot of grass like a penthouse roof. I had never seen traces of a large stone barn built straight on to a farmhouse before, and I was interested. I supposed that rats had made it inconvenient to have a barn on to the house, and that it had been destroyed and a garden made on its floor space; though why later farmers had abandoned the garden I could not imagine – still less why they had erected that wall between the grass plot and the house.

Mrs. Stokes returned with the key. She still looked "put about," as country people say, and I apologised for putting her to the trouble of opening the place.

"Oh, it isn't any trouble, sir," she said, as she fitted the key into the big lock. "Only – well, I'll tell you the truth, sir," she burst out suddenly, standing upright and facing me. "They do say as this place isn't – chancy. It's not the farm, it's just this one place. That's why they've walled it off. I don't know nothing myself," she added hastily. "I come from Dorset myself, and I've never heard nor seen a thing. But my husband's people, they've farmed this land for centuries, so they say, and there's not one of 'em as'll go anigh this plot."

"Is there a story about it?" I asked. I am very keen on folk-lore and legends, and thought there might be something here.

"N-no," she answered, rather reluctantly. And then, "But if I was you, sir, I'd keep out o' Simmel Acres Plot."

"Well, let's look at it, anyway," I said; and with no more words we opened the door – the lock shrieked dismally, I remember – and went in.

It was by no means as bad as Mrs. Stokes had painted it. The grass was long and rank, but the nettles had confined themselves to the shelter of the high stone walls. But the thing that drew my attention was the old gabled end of the barn. It was perhaps sixteen feet high, rounded off in a curiously rough and archaic form of arch. The roof, as I have said, projected in a kind of rugged penthouse, about two feet deep, and about half-way up the wall there was a niche with a stone bust of a man.

It was a very odd piece of work, worn by time and exposure, but quite complete enough for me. The top part of the head was the most disfigured; I could see some kind of fillet or crown, and some clumsy, conventional indications of hair. The blank eye-sockets were rather large, oddly rounded at the corners, and had in consequence an expression of ruthlessness. The nose was too worn to be in any way remarkable; but the mouth had the most subtle expression – at once cynical, suffering, cruel, undaunted and callous. The chin was square, but weak; the neck powerful, in a conventional manner. It was altogether a remarkable thing – almost savage in its clumsiness and crudity, and yet conveying a singular impression of truth to an original.

At first I thought it was a piece of decadent Roman sculpture; then I dismissed that as absurd. How could a Roman bust be in a barn in the Cotswolds? It might have been an eighteenth century copy, but I didn't think so; it was too crude, too strong, too – I must use the word again – too archaic. Besides, when the eighteenth century copied Roman busts they were put in little pseudo-classical temples, not in niches in barns.

This was not all. Below the barn was a small semi-circular basin, floored with smooth pebbles, through which welled up water so clear as to be almost invisible – exactly like the Holy Wishing Wells one finds occasionally, decorated with pins and rags and other tributes to the presiding deity. But here there were no offerings.

The loveliness of the morning was even more apparent in the little enclosure. The soft sky gained colour from the grey walls, the grass smelt fresh and wet, the water mirrored the tiny white clouds. It was exactly the place for an invalid, I thought, restful, open and quiet. I told Mrs. Stokes my decision, and she protested no more.

Together we brought the sofa out into the plot; and Markham and I settled down there for the morning.

We had set the sofa against the farmhouse wall, at the end of the little plot away from the old barn-end with its bubbling spring. When he was established I went into the house for some books and notes – I had a lot of work to do that vac. – and it was some minutes before I came out again. When I did, I noticed that Markham was not lying, as he should have been, flat on his back; he had rolled over on to his side and was staring with a frowning, puzzled look at the bust above the well.

"Hullo," I said, "oughtn't you to be on your back?"

He paid no attention. Indeed, I don't think he heard me. He was muttering something, like a man trying to remember a half-forgotten phrase.

"Damn it all, how did it go?" he broke out suddenly. "'*Et te simulacrum... Et te...*' Damn it! What was it?"

"What was what?" I asked, putting my books down on the table.

He looked round at me, and his face cleared a little.

"I – something came into my head – a sentence or something... I can't remember. I read it once – or heard it – when I was a kid... Some old book that belonged to some bloomin' ancestor. Dashed if I can remember... *Et te simulacrum...* Curse it! How did it go?"

"What about it?" I asked.

Again he made no answer – just lay, frowning a little and muttering. At last he said,

"What is it written under that head over there?"

"Under the bust? Nothing."

"There is," he insisted. "What is it?"

Just to satisfy him I went and looked. He was quite right – there were words there.

"There is something," I said, "but I can't read it. I can only see bits of words here and there – nothing consecutive. *Simul*, I think that is–"

"*Simulacrum, et te – requiro...*" muttered Markham.

I was very much surprised – for several reasons. First I was surprised that he should be interested at all; then that he should be quoting, however scrappily, a Latin sentence; and last that he could see that there was an inscription, let alone read the words. Kneeling on the ground before it, I could only just make out the defaced letters; and he was twenty yards away, lying flat.

"Can you read it right over there?" I called in astonishment.

"No – is it written there?" he cried back, wriggling round eagerly. "Read it out, Norton – I can't remember how it goes."

"I can't make out more than a word or two," I said. "And I don't know all the words – must be late Latin, I think. *Simul* – or perhaps you're right, *simulacrum* – something about water – and I think that's *lunae* – and – no, I can't read it."

Markham seemed dissatisfied.

"There's more of it than that," he insisted.

"Yes, there is," I agreed, "but it's so worn. But, I say, how did you know what it was? How did you know it was there?"

He looked puzzled.

"Damned if I know," he began. He spoke slowly, like a man groping for words, or for ideas. "I just knew... We come from these parts, you know... used to have a big place in the eighteenth century, or something. Rather rips, I believe we were – Hellfire Club and all that tosh..."

He suddenly broke off. He made a quick gesture, like that of a man who remembers. His face cleared and his eyes shone. His lips moved a little as if he had caught the words he had been seeking.

"Got it?" I asked. I was rather thrilled; it was, I thought, a very interesting example of an inherited memory – something long forgotten and now recalled by equally forgotten associations.

He made no reply, so I asked again – "Remembered it?"

He looked up at me, grinning, and wouldn't answer. It was a queer look, half ashamed, half malicious, wholly triumphant. Every now and then throughout that morning I caught him moving his lips as if he were repeating something he was anxious not to forget – like an amateur actor learning his part – and there was an odd, excited air about him like that of a small boy with a mischievous secret. He looked as if he were up to something recklessly silly, like an extra mad "Cupper" rag. Of course I knew he couldn't be really, but I felt uneasy somehow. He'd always had the reputation for such daredevil games, and though he was tied to his couch he might be all the more restless, planning any monkey tricks. And he had a mocking light in his eye that irritated me badly. I know I'm not his type, but open mockery was a bit more than I could stick. I decided I'd leave him to himself in the afternoon and clear out for a good walk on my own.

He seemed quite pleased when I mentioned this. All he said was, just as I looked in to the little enclosure to say I was starting,

"Right. I say, you might just give me a drink before you go, will you? Some of that spring by the wall there."

I said I'd go in and get him a drink; the spring looked good enough, but you never know, especially near a farmyard. But that wouldn't do him at all. He wanted the water from that well and nothing else. And when I said I wouldn't get it for him, he actually moved as if to get up and get it for himself.

Well, he wasn't a kid. He knew the risks of drinking the stuff as well as I did; so, still protesting, I scooped up about a spoonful of the water for him.

"I want to drink the old lad's health," he said, half apologetically, when I handed it to him; and he held the glass up as if he really were drinking a health, and muttered some more nonsense about "libatio aquae." It was too low for me to hear, and anyhow I was fed up with his nonsense. He still had the daring, wild expression I'd noticed in the morning, and he grinned at me in an absolutely impish way. I cleared out, annoyed and just a trifle uneasy.

I enjoyed my walk. Markham had ruffled me, and it was a real relief to be by myself for a bit. We hadn't anything in common, really. I'm a plodder by nature, and I had no sympathy with his wild outbursts of spirits and the mad enterprises that he alternated with training of a rigorous kind. Even since his illness, when we had seen a good deal of each other, I had never understood him much. I'd been surprised, for instance, to hear him quote Latin simply because I had taken it for granted that he was the ordinary beefy, brainless type; but I realised now that I had not the smallest reason, really, to think so. I knew nothing, quite literally nothing, of his mind. I began thinking of his queer behaviour that morning – his puzzled face, his relief at remembering some half-forgotten tag of dog-Latin seen in an old book, the dancing mockery of his eyes, that absurd business of the "libation." I began to wonder how long our companionship would last, and I thought that probably it would not be very long. There, at least, I was right.

I got in about six, perhaps a little earlier. I know dusk had not yet fallen; but the warmth was gone from the air, and the shadows were chill. I went out to the little grass plot at once to see if Markham had been moved in yet. I thought it might be risky for him after his illness to be lying out so late when April was not yet in.

He was still there, lying flat and rigid under the grey rug on the couch; and the dim colour of the rug and the stillness of his pose gave me quite a shock. He didn't look alive at all; he looked like a figure carved in grey stone on a tomb. It was the merest momentary impression, but for the instant it seemed to me as if even his face was fixed. And there was something else about it...

Then he opened his eyes and looked at me with the dazed sort of look a man has when he wakes suddenly – puzzled, rather appealing – you know what I mean, rather childlike somehow. And I suddenly had the oddest sort of guilty feeling, as if I'd been thinking something treacherous – planning some evil to him – I can't explain, it was all so vague, mixed up with that swiftly-lost impression of his set, still face and figure, like a debased statue on an evil tomb.

We had a door between our rooms in the farm. At first I used to leave it ajar, in case Markham should wake and want some small attention; but that night I closed it. I can't explain why, for I'd quite lost the irritation I'd felt earlier in the day; instead I had a queer sort of feeling, equally irrational, of pity, almost of grief; and yet I shut the door with a feeling of half-shamed relief such as one feels when one leaves a mourner one can't help.

I woke quite suddenly. Perhaps it was the big, bright moon, nearly full for Easter, that awakened me; but I had the impression that it was a voice. I sat up and listened. I thought I could hear it again – a voice (or was it two voices?) speaking quick and quiet in the next room.

"Want anything, Markham?" I called and my voice sounded odd – anxious, and a little unsteady.

There was immediate and deathly silence – the kind of silence that follows on a furtive sound. I strained my ears to listen. I remember now how the flood of strong moonlight washed my room, and the look of the queer, sharp shadows that edged it. I could hear my own heart beating in the dead silence.

Nothing – not a whisper, not a rustle. Only that strained, aching, unnatural void, so different from real quiet, that you hear when you listen intently.

I waited a little, more uneasy than I liked to admit. I had, half unconsciously, in my mind the vision of Markham as I had seen him that afternoon, grey and rigid, with a set, altered, familiar, dreadful face...

I twisted my legs round over the edge of my bed. The room had that half-familiar, half-magic look you get in full moonlight – solid and yet ethereal, real and still dreamlike... I felt as if minutes passed in that dead, unnatural silence. It took more effort than I should have imagined possible to break through it.

"Markham!" I said again; and, though I pitched my voice low, it sounded horribly loud. It cracked upwards unexpectedly; and I knew then – and not till then – that I was – terrified.

No sound. Only the echo of that breaking, frightened, stranger's voice that had come from my own dry throat.

I got up and opened the door between our rooms.

The window, uncurtained, let the moonlight stream in. The shadows were massive, hard-edged, like odd shapes cut in a solid substance. I could see the bed, a patchwork of black and white, cut by the shadows of things in the room. One shadow was humped, rounded – I thought it moved, and spun round to see what threw it. There was nothing. When I turned back it had gone. Perhaps it had never been there...

The pillow was, as it were, cut off from the whiteness of the bed by the straight, solid shadow of the curtain hanging beside the window. I could just see dimly in the blackness the blacker blot made by Markham's head. He lay as motionless as stone...

I stood there in the chequered black and white. I don't think I *thought* at all. I just stood there, resisting with all my strength a wave of sheer panic that swept over me. It was as if in that silent room I stood on the verge of something too evil, too fearful, to understand. I could see nothing, hear nothing, but I felt evil, malignant, appalling, in the very air. And then quite silently the curtain at the window waved in some mysterious breath of night air – lifted for a second, and fell as silently. But in that single instant I had seen...

Markham's head lay as if carved in stone on the pillow; the eyes were blankly lidded, the features altered – something twisted in the roughened hair, like a fillet – he smiled a little, an enigmatic, cruel and anguished smile... Markham, yet not Markham...

I forget what happened. A black wave seemed to engulf me. I heard the rush of it in my ears – I couldn't breathe for it... Then I was standing in my own room, backing up to the open window, deadly cold, seeing that dreadful face. And then panic seized me – not for myself, but for Markham. What had happened? He was helpless... I must go back – must help him – I couldn't let It...

If there had been some sound it wouldn't have been so bad. A groan, a cry for help, even a whisper would have been more – more human. I should have known then that Markham really was there...

I lit a candle. It took me, I knew, a very long time, I fumbled so. But at last I had a warm, friendly light instead of the mocking fantasy of moonlight. I went back.

The room looked just as usual. Markham lay, his brows a little drawn down, his mouth a little open, as if he were puzzled or expostulating – but it was Markham. There was no doubt of that. I felt a warm gush of sheer relief as I saw his familiar face. Oddly enough, I didn't, even then, feel at all ashamed of my terror. There *had* been something wrong, something appalling, ghastly, in that room. It was gone now, but it had been there...

I went back to bed, but I did not sleep again. I listened, achingly, for a sound that never came.

I felt oddly embarrassed at the idea of meeting Markham in

the morning. It was as if I had unwittingly surprised him in some secret, shameful and intimate. And I noticed that he, too, when we met, seemed unwilling to meet my eye. We were both conscious of something – some bond of knowledge that was at the same time a bar. And I think we both wondered what the other knew.

After a pretence of a meal I tried, feebly enough, to get something out of him.

"I don't think you'd better go out today," I said, looking at him straight.

He changed colour at once.

"What d'you mean?" he asked, almost defiantly.

"I mean," I said – carefully, because I wasn't myself sure of my own meaning – "that I think Mrs. Stokes is right. That enclosure isn't – healthy."

He laughed, rather a mirthless, sneering sound.

"Too late to think of that now," he said; and as our eyes met I saw a difference – his face looked strange, yet familiar, with its cynical, suffering mouth and expressionless eyes.

"Markham!" I cried, dropping all pretence. "Markham – what is it? What have you done? Can't we..?"

My voice died away.

He had said nothing. His whole face was set, rigid in that blank, cynical, anguished look. It was as if stricken to stone before my eyes. We sat, the spring sun on us, facing each other in horror and despair.

I said no more. I knew he was right – it was too late to avoid the enclosure, with its well and terrible bust. I stayed with Markham all that day, pretending to read as he lay motionless and silent in the air and sunshine of that haunted plot called Simmel Acres. I was tense the whole time, listening with strained ears, stealing furtive glances now at Markham's set face, now at the marred bust above the clear water of the spring. But nothing happened, except that once I thought I saw on the grass near the couch a crouching shadow... It was not there when I looked sharply up. I had imagined it, perhaps.

But as evening drew on I felt we could not leave it like that. We must do something.

"Markham," I said, as firmly as I could, "I think I'd better sleep in your room tonight."

He said nothing. He only turned his head a little and looked at me.

"You were restless last night," I said feebly. "You might need me."

"*Restless?*" he half whispered, mockery in his tone.

I remembered that rigid form and terrible set face.

"You might need me," I repeated.

"No. It's decent of you, Norton – but – no. I-I'd rather you didn't – I mean – I'm better alone."

I don't know what made me say it.

"Where did you get the words from?" I asked.

He stared at me as if he would read my thoughts.

"*I don't know,*" he whispered; and his whole face was suddenly transfigured with sheer appalling panic. "Norton – Norton," he babbled, clutching at me, "if I knew! If only I knew! I might find others – to undo it – Norton, can't you think? Where can I find out? What was the book?"

I was immensely relieved. It was far less dreadful put into words.

"I'll find out," I said boldly. "There'll be books – people must know... I'll ask old Henderson, he's always working at these things, rites and old magic and things. He'll know, Markham, sure to. I'll go over to Oxford first thing tomorrow..."

"No! No! Tonight, Norton, it must be tonight. The moon's full tonight. You must, you simply must. You don't know – I-I can't..."

He was nearly beside himself.

"I will," I promised. "I'll go now. I'll be in Oxford before eight. I'll find Henderson. It'll be all right, Markham, he's sure to know. It'll be all right..."

I shall never forget that mad journey to Oxford. I cycled, as there was no quicker way to go; and it took me two hours, panting up hills, sweating as if I were on an errand of life and death. It was, I knew, even more serious than that... And I had no clue – nothing but that Markham's family had once been connected with the village – that some ancestor had worshipped with the Hellfire Club... that there had been a book... Would it, could it be the faintest use? Could old Henderson – could anyone, pedant or priest, help us?

It seemed hours and hours before I got into the long roads of conventional houses that lie like a web about Oxford. The clocks were striking nine as I reached Carfax.

Henderson was away. Of course he was, in the vac. I stood stunned as the porter carefully explained it to me – I think he thought I was drunk. I could not take it in. Our last chance! The porter saw that it was something serious.

"Something urgent was it, sir?" he asked at last.

"Yes," I whispered. My lips were almost too dry to speak.

"Well, sir – seein' as it's urgent... Mr. 'Enderson 'as a little 'ouse out near Kingston Bagpuize. 'E don't like visitors there, not in vacation but seein' as it's urgent... It ain't on the 'phone but if you'd care to run out..."

I was down the steps before he finished. He shouted the name of the house after me as I raced off. The moon, moving majestically and remorselessly up the sky filled me with desperation. I should never, never be in time...

I don't know what I said to Henderson. I thought I should never make him understand. I don't now why he listened – why he didn't write me down as mad, or drunk. But, thank God, he didn't; he made me sit down and drink something – I don't know what, I couldn't taste it, and my hands were shaking so that I couldn't drink without spilling the stuff – while he listened and nodded and consulted old books. He moved with the slowness of a very old man, taking down one book after another, consulting manuscripts, reading passages, while the minutes ticked away and the night crept on... I can see him now, so old and bent, with his careful gestures clear in the steady lamplight, and the smell of old books in the air...

The clocks were striking eleven as we rushed, in a hired car, out of the dim Oxford streets and struck up the glimmering white road to Simmel Acres Farm. I don't think we said a word. I know I sat with every muscle taut, straining with impatience, wild hope alternating with despair as I watched the moon rise higher and higher in the clear sky. We should never do it!

The moon was almost at the zenith when at last we reached the farm. I could not stand when I got out – old Henderson had to put his hand under my arm to keep me from falling.

I was making for the door, but he stopped me.

"No," he said, "the enclosure – the well. We must go there."

He was muttering to himself, like a man saying prayers, but I knew that he was not praying to any Christian God.

The outer door was shut, but the key was in the lock, and we opened it easily.

The little yard looked quite empty. The royal moonlight flooded the young grass and the trees with leaves just unfolding. Only at the end the penthouse of stone threw a dark, menacing shadow. Beneath it came the tiny tinkle of water in the stone-edged spring. And, half in the shadow, half in the moonlight, I saw Markham lying – Markham, with a white, set face turned up to the moon. And his face was that of the sneering bust above him.

"WILL YE NO' COME BACK AGAIN?"

THE friends of Annis Breck (who were not many, and were all female) generally spoke with respect of her Sound Good Sense, her Practical Ability and her Capabilities. Her foes (who were more, but still not many) said that she was hard, commercial and unimaginative. Every one else said that you could never really *know* Miss Breck, she was so — and left it at that. Her idea of opening a hostel for working girls in Burley was, everyone agreed, just like her, though they said so for different reasons. She had done so much, one way and another, for girls. Women and their rights (or, more often, wrongs) had always been her strong point; and of course, added the foes, she always had a keen eye to the main chance. If Annis Breck took up a thing, you might be pretty sure there was money in it. She'd make this hostel a very paying thing, see if she didn't. But when they heard that she had taken Queen's Garth, they wondered if she would. They then said that these "business women"...! and again left it at that.

For, they pointed out, Queen's Garth had stood empty for years. It had been unfortunate in its owners. The last of the original family, old Miss Campbell, was the only survivor of a clan that had lived in the house ever since it was built in the seventeenth century. They had apparently specialised in strong-minded females, who had very occasionally condescended to marry, but had always ruled with a rod of iron, having a deep-rooted suspicion of men and a determination to keep them well under. How they had ever married at all was a marvel; no doubt it had been entirely for practical, and never for romantic, reasons. The family had now died out, it was true, but (said the foes, nastily) it seemed that the tradition of the firm female and the rod of iron was to endure. They pitied the girls, they said.

Then came the friends. Annis was wonderful, they knew that, but had she really *considered*? Did she realise all it *meant*? The house had stood empty so long. The furniture, they knew, had been lovely – Sheraton and Chippendale and all sorts of gems – but it must be simply dropping to pieces now. The house was charming, of course, and dirt cheap, and the rooms beautifully large, but, my *dear! Think* of the work, with all those stairs and twisting passages, and no conveniences to speak of. Besides, there was some story – oh, no one *believed it*, of course, but you know what maids *are*. They'd turn every echo and waving curtain into a ghost. And water, always such a problem in these picturesque old places... Still, Annis probably knew best. Practical, dear Annis!

Annis herself felt not the smallest doubt as to her venture. She never did, which, no doubt, was why so many of them succeeded. She took Queen's Garth as soon as she saw it, stairs and ghost and water and all. She did not underrate these disadvantages, but she simply accepted them because she knew as soon as she saw the old red house that she "belonged". Almost unconsciously she felt that; she closed her bargain on the spot.

She meant to open the hostel on New Year's Day. Alterations must be made, of course, and equally of course they would not be made in time unless she personally saw that they were. You could never trust men to keep their word. So she moved, early in December, into Queen's Garth, to keep an eye on the men, make curtains, and so on, and arrange everything properly. Organisation, she said, was the key to success. Anything could be done by good organisation.

She said this to Lucy Ferrars, an old friend of W.S.P.U. days who had called to ask Annis to speak at a meeting. Lucy was always getting up meetings and asking Annis to speak at them, and Annis was always irritated sooner or later by Lucy's absolute lack of the power to organise. Her meetings were never successful. So she repeated her formula about the necessity of organisation, *àpropos* of the hostel, but hoping that Lucy would take it to heart. Apparently she didn't – Annis thought it was that she wouldn't.

"How *marv'lous* you are," was all that she said in the bleating voice that irritated Annis so badly. "Marv'lous. And what *perfect* furniture, Annis. So quaint."

Miss Breck shuddered.

"I s'pose you've got it all in here," pursued Lucy.

Annis gave up the hope of impressing her with the necessity of organisation, and allowed the talk to turn to furniture.

"Oh, no," she replied, bored but tolerant. "The house is practically all furnished, and it's all eighteenth century stuff."

"My *dear!* It must have cost you a *fortune!*" gasped Lucy.

"Not a bit of it. No one wanted it. You see, the furniture goes with the house. Some clause in the old lady's will – seems it was the rule in the family. It makes it awfully – personal," she added, half to herself, passing her fingers lightly over the back of an elegant Chippendale chair. "It's very lucky for me," she went on, smiling dryly, "that people are so idiotically superstitious. I should never have got the house otherwise..."

She broke off, turning her head sharply.

"What is it?" breathed Lucy, her prominent eyes goggling, her mouth gaping.

"Nothing," said Annis, relaxing her attitude. "I thought I saw someone – a reflection in my glasses, no doubt. For the moment I thought one of the men had come back... You'll stay and have some tea, won't you, Lucy? Bachelor's Hall, of course, but I make myself very comfortable."

"Are you all alone?" asked Lucy, still round-eyed.

"Oh, yes. No sense in having maids for one person – especially as I hear they're going to be hard to keep! But I can cook, you know. You will stay, won't you?"

"Oh, no, thank you very much," said Lucy hastily. "I – it's getting late – it's dark so very early now. I have such a lot to do – this meeting, you know – I *think* I must go, dear, thank you so much..."

She babbled all the way to the door, and annoyed Annis very much by stopping on the threshold, half in and half out, to press her to come and sleep with her until the house should be ready and there were "girls and maids and people" for company. She gave no reason for this suggestion – Lucy, Annis reflected with amusement, didn't know the meaning of the word "reason" – but was very persistent and incoherent. Annis got rid of her with difficulty.

It was nearly dark when she turned back into the house. She made it a rule to go the rounds of all the rooms each night, to make sure that there were no open windows or smouldering cigarette ends ("You know what men are!") – and now, thanks to Lucy's maunderings, she would have to do this by the inadequate light of an electric torch, since candles carried in the hand were hardly safe. She thought, as she tripped over forgotten and unnecessary steps and felt her way along the winding passages, that the house was more inconvenient than she had thought. Odd that, with all its twists and turns, it should somehow seem familiar. One would soon get used to its irregularities. And the girls wouldn't mind. Girls, she reflected bitterly, never mind anything really badly. Girls were what men had made them – giddy, fickle, heartless. They had found that faith and loyalty and depth of feeling didn't pay – thanks to men.

"*Men!*" she muttered aloud, slamming a door. "*Men!* All alike! just use women and throw them away – forget they exist. No wonder girls…"

She stopped short. A tiny sound, like the faint echo of a sob, caught her ear.

She stood, listening intently. No – not a sound. Or – yes, there it was again – a sound of muffled, pitiful, hopeless crying.

For a moment she stood there, straining every sense. Then suddenly relief swept over her; "It's a child," she thought. "Some child who's brought one of the men his tea, and got left behind… It was just here somewhere."

She walked briskly down the passage, making encouraging sounds, opening every door, examining every room, flashing the beam of her torch into every corner. The house was empty and still.

"Very odd," thought Annis, annoyed. "It must have been some

trick of the wind."

And she finished her rounds and went back to her cosy little sitting-room, with its Georgian furniture and Victorian silhouettes, to study catalogues and reports. She spent a peaceful and busy evening, and slept extra well in consequence.

The morning was sunny and mild, and Annis seized the opportunity to go over the garden, which she had not yet investigated, with a view to turning it to the best advantage for "her girls." The lawns should be cut and rolled and turned into courts for tennis and badminton; the gravelled courtyard outside the old stables would be excellent for netball; she might fix up fives in the stables themselves. And she would leave bits of real garden simply for rest. She would keep the old flower-borders, with their fragrant hedges of rosemary and lavender and lad's love. Rosemary, that's for remembrance. And lad's love – there was some song about it –

> *"What is lad's love and the love of a lad?*
> *Lad's love is green and gray;*
> *And the love of a lad is merry and sad*
> *Here yesterday – gone today.*
> *Heigh-ho, hey!*
> *Here yesterday – gone today!"*

Yes, there was something melancholy, as well as sweet, about lad's love. Perhaps that should go...

But the old rose-garden, with its formal beds and stone seats and sundial, must certainly remain. She liked the sundial. It would have a motto, she was sure – "Time flieth, hope dieth" – why did the words come into her head? She had not seen them anywhere that she remembered.

She strolled across. Yes, she was right. The words were almost obliterated, worn and over-grown with moss, but they were there. She leant over the slab, tracing them with an idle finger.

"Time flieth, hope..."

Annis suddenly stiffened. She remained, her hands resting lightly on the old stone slab, her eyes bent on the motto; but she, too, might have been carved in stone. For she felt, as certainly as she had ever felt anything, that someone stood behind her, reading the words over her shoulder – someone sneering, hating, despising her... She could hear her pulses beating in her throat – she could not breathe...

And then, as suddenly, these symptoms passed. She was alone in the winter sunshine, and a robin sang sweet and shrill in the bare rose-trees. She drew a deep breath, looked slowly round her, and walked thoughtfully into the house.

It was some time before she threw off the impression of those few seconds; but when she did she was very much ashamed of herself, and in consequence very angry.

"*Idiot!*" she said crossly to herself. "Been overdoing it, I suppose, like all the other fools... I'll go to bed early tonight."

It was Saturday, and the workmen went early, so Annis was able to make her rounds in the bleak light of a winter afternoon. She looked very carefully through each room, and then locked it. She wasn't going to have the trouble she'd had last night over that imaginary child. She'd make sure, this time, that every room was empty before she locked it – the big bedrooms with the old four-poster beds, the little slip of a room with the spinet, the pale old drawing-room that still smelt faintly of pot-pourri – she examined and locked them all.

What a lot of rooms there were! – and each with some trace of occupation. Why, in this one there was an old-fashioned work-table with needlework still in it, the needle rusted into the stuff! How could people ever have done that endless, jigsaw patchwork, she wondered as she took it up. But how pretty some of the stuffs had been! Those scraps of blue silk with tiny bright posies – charming. She touched the silk lovingly. Then she stood, her fingers stiffening, listening intently.

The spinet. Quite unmistakably she heard the faltering, tinkling notes of unpractised fingers – scales, broken by false notes, or ending abruptly. In the pauses there came little sobbing sounds... Annis stood motionless in the gathering dusk, her cold fingers clutching the old, old patchwork, listening to the faint, jingling notes of the spinet in the locked room next door...

The sound changed. There was a jangle, as if the performer had dropped weary hands from the keys; and then, very slowly and uncertainly, there came an air, picked out with one faltering hand – the old, plaintive, haunting tune, "Will ye no' come back again?"

It, too, broke off half finished, and again there came the sound of hopeless, muffled weeping...

Or was it rain? Rain was pattering softly on the windows. There was no other sound except the beating of her own heart...

Annis thrust the old patchwork back into the table. She ran, stumbling, to the door, locked it behind her, fled back to her own little sanctum, and locked herself in. She stood leaning against the door, breathing hard and unevenly, her hand still on the latch.

What was that – that pale figure facing her, with wide, staring dark eyes in a white face... Only herself, reflected in the panel mirror opposite the door. For a moment it had looked different... But it was only herself, Annis Breck, white-faced, with staring, frightened eyes...

She crossed to the hearth and sat down. She was trembling violently. She sat looking with some surprise at her own shaking hands. The rain beat softly on the windows, melancholy and persistent. The grey, rain-swept garden sighed in the evening wind.

Annis rose, rather unsteadily, and went across to put up the shutters. The garden was so sad, grey in the rain. The sundial glimmered in the dusk. Was that – ? No, only a mist-wreath curving about the dial – it has dissolved already. But oh, how dreary, how melancholy! She put up the old white shutters hurriedly, and at an incredibly early hour sought the comfort and security of her bed.

Annis awoke with a start. What was it that had awakened her? Surely she had heard something. Was it a voice? A name, echoing in her ears? Or was it the spinet – "Will ye no' come back again?" *"Time flieth, hope dieth."* Yes – and a girl – a girl dressed in a frock of blue silk, patterned with tiny gay posies – a girl at the spinet – a girl by the sundial, tracing the sad old motto, while slow tears dropped on the stone slab – a girl called Annis...

The girl had her own face. She understood it now. And his name – ah, how had she ever forgotten it? – his name had been Richard...

THE OLD LADY

ADELA YOUNG must have come up to Oxford at the same time as myself; but no one, in a way, knew that she had. She was one of those people whom one never notices, physically or mentally – the kind of person whose adjectives you always qualify with "-ish." She was smallish, thinnish, palish, with dim brownish hair and pale scared eyes. She had a timid, withdrawing manner; she dressed always in rather dismal neutral tints – dull greys and dim greens and fawnish drab, and tussore silk, to match her sallow skin. She was a good deal ignored.

I should never have known Adela, or the old lady, if it hadn't been for a silly bet. One does these things in one's first year – risky, futile, daring things – rather caddish things sometimes – with perhaps half-a-crown on them. Someone had ragged me on my numerous acquaintances, and I'd retorted by saying that anyone could make friends with anyone else if they wanted to. Maude Evans caught me up at once.

"Rot!" she said, with her usual affectation of breezy brusquerie. "There's some people no one would ever know."

"I bet there's nobody in College I couldn't get to know if I wanted to," I asserted, with more assurance than was at all warranted. Maude had that effect on me.

Maude thought rapidly. I could see her, as I watched her challengingly, going over all the various types of people – the superior, the literary, the sporting, the fashionable, the "swots." I felt pretty safe. I was only a fresher, but I had possibilities of friendships with all these types.

"You'd never get to know little Whatshername– that washed-out little dishcloth – Young, that's it. I bet you'd never get thick with *her.*"

I had my doubts too, really. It was like betting you'd quarrel with a sofa-cushion. But of course I took her on.

"Bet I will," I said at once.

"How much?" Maude caught me up. She always had rather an eye to the main chance.

"Oh – what you like." I expected the usual half-crown.

"Bet you a fiver you don't."

That stung me. Maude would never have risked such a sum – five pounds means a good deal to a girl undergraduate – if she hadn't felt certain of winning.

"Right," I said immediately.

Then we settled the terms of the bet. I was to have invited and been invited – the latter was, of course, the important point – to six walks or meals by the end of the term: to have got some sort of real confidence ("heart to heart talk," we called it) out of little Young, and have wangled an invitation to stay at her home before the end of the next term – the summer term.

Even as I took it on I felt a good deal of a cad. I felt much worse when I began the campaign. The college invitations were all right – one could take them as meaning a lot or as meaning nothing; but to fish for confidences and try to secure an invitation to stay with her people – rotten, both of them. I felt dimly even then that, even when tiresome, both are honours – often the highest honours one person can do another. But I'd been dared. Much as I wanted to win five pounds from the comparatively wealthy Maude Evans, little as I liked the idea of parting with any of my much smaller income to her, what really *mattered* was that I had been challenged and had accepted the challenge. So I set about the siege of Adela Young.

It was extremely difficult. Maude couldn't have chosen a more hopeless subject. Certainly if I could "make good" with her I could

with anyone, I thought, as I studied her across the dinner table
that night. She looked permanently scared – she hardly raised her
voice above a whisper, and her remarks, when audible, were merely
hurried agreements with whatever the last speaker had said. She
was silent whenever possible; her very movements were furtive
and rapid, as if she had to get through the meal against time, and
secretly. For the first time I felt rather *intriguée* about her. Plain,
awkward, nondescript as she was, I felt something unusual, almost
mysterious, about her. I was even rather thrilled by the idea of
finding out more about her.

I caught her up as she was silently scuttling to her room after
dinner – I remembered, now that I came to think of it, that she
almost never waited for coffee after dinner, nor, indeed, for any
semi-social function like that.

"I say," I said, overtaking her, "you're taking Mods. this term,
aren't you?"

"Y-Yes," she breathed, looking terrified.

"I wonder if I might come in and go over the Plato with you?"

She said nothing, just goggled at me.

"You are taking the Plato set books, aren't you?"

"Oh, yes."

"I thought so. I've seen you at the classes."

"Yes."

We seemed stuck. I tried again.

"I meant to go over the stuff with Hanson and Phil Leamore,
but they say they aren't going to revise at all. Shall you?"

"Oh, yes."

"When are you going to go over the Plato?"

She looked at me mutely, her mouth opening and shutting like
a newly caught fish. She seemed quite incapable of making any
suggestion.

"Could you possibly do it tonight?"

"Oh, yes."

I began to wonder if she *could* say anything except "Yes" and "Oh,
yes."

"Then may I come along now?" I pressed on.

She said nothing but opened her door for me. She had the oddest manner as she did it – reluctant, almost, and yet half anxious. I wondered rather cockily if she was one of those people you meet sometimes who, when they want a thing, are half afraid of getting it.

As we entered I looked curiously round to see what ideas of decoration such a person (or thing – she hardly seemed to be a real person) would have. She had apparently none. Not a picture, not a flower, not a cushion or a novel or a vase or a photograph was there. Just the usual regulation college furniture and the set books for Pass Mods. I've seldom seen anything so chilling, so absolutely impersonal. I began to regret the bet. Maude Evans was probably right – there were people you could never get to know, because there was nothing to know; and Adela Young was one of them. She had a nondescript face and figure, and inside – nothing. Nothing at all. However I'd undertaken it and I'd go on. I sat down – on a stiff college chair – you couldn't somehow sit naturally on the floor in that dead-alive room – and opened the "Apology" of Plato.

It was exactly like working with a well-informed gramophone – a hushed, husky voice with nothing alive behind it. But she'd quite obviously worked a lot. She was most useful. While we were working it wasn't so bad. But when I tried to get cheery and conversational afterwards – suggested making tea and so on – she was as palely noncommittal as ever. "Yes" – "No" – "Thank you" – "No, thank you" – "Yes" – "Yes, please" – "Oh, yes" – "Yes..." That was about the extent of it. But the very difficulty of it determined me. I fixed up a second tête-à-tête, and went away feeling quite astonishingly curious. She puzzled me completely. Pallid and dull and dusty and silent as she was, she somehow suggested a mystery. I found myself thinking of her constantly. She absorbed my thoughts as did no one else in the place, however brilliant or beautiful or witty. I could not get her out of my mind.

There wasn't much left of that term – only a few days – but I managed to see quite a lot of Adela Young. But "see" is the right verb. I saw her – occasionally heard her colourless voice whispering Greek verbs or Latin constructions – and that was all. I began to feel rather alarmed for my fiver. I didn't see how anyone could *ever* extract any confidences from that cobweb of a girl. I didn't believe she had any to make. As to an invitation from her people – hopeless. You simply couldn't imagine her as having any people or home or anything. I wondered vaguely, when I first thought of this, if she could be a foundling, a child from some orphanage or something, and, if so, whether that wouldn't cancel the bet. I rather jumped at the idea – I thought it would solve my difficulties so very nicely. So, rather tentatively, I broached the subject of families and homes and vacation plans to Adela.

"Shall you spend all the vac. at home?" I asked her one night when we'd "gone over" the work for the next day's paper – Tacitus, I think it was.

"Oh, yes."

"Shall you stay up for the viva, or go home in between?"

"Go home, I think." She paused, and then actually volunteered a remark. "I come so late on the list," she added.

"Yes. So do I, of course. Nuisance, beginning with a Y. But it's too expensive to go all the way to Ireland and back again. I shall have to stay up. Sickening," I added, "I shall be the only person in coll. except the dons."

That was as broad as I dared make it, but I began to fear that she wouldn't take the hint, she was so long before she spoke. She gave me the impression that she was trying to make up her mind to do something rather dreadful. At last she brought it out.

"I – that is, my guardian – she said – I mean, I – we – should be so glad – she said, if I had any friend – who would care..."

Her voice died away. It had been even more gasping and husky than usual – as if she were forcing herself to speak and her strength or courage wouldn't last out.

It wasn't exactly what you might call an invitation, but I eagerly took it as such.

"D'you mean that I could stay with you till the viva?" I asked with indecent haste.

"Oh, yes. She – she'd like you to..." Again her voice faded into silence.

"But does she know anything about me?" I asked.

"She wants me – make friends – my own age..." whispered Adela. She said nothing whatever, I noticed, about her own inclinations.

I twisted round – (we were in my room, and I was sitting on the floor, while Adela Young sat in an upright chair behind me) – I twisted round and looked at her curiously. Her face was dead white and her forehead was damp. Her pale eyes stared at me, terrified, above a handkerchief that she held with a shaking hand to her mouth.

What on *earth* could the girl be so scared about? At the very worst, I might be horribly rude – though she must have known me well enough to know that I shouldn't be. But I couldn't even then see how the grossest insolence could be as terrifing as that.

"Did she – your guardian – suggest that you should ask me?" I asked, curious.

She nodded dumbly.

"It's *awfully* kind of her," I said warmly. "I'd love to."

I expected to see her face clear at that; but it didn't. She looked as scared as ever, mutely terrified, with a kind of half-wistful, almost pitying look as well. I stared at her, rather obviously, I'm afraid, trying to think what the idea was that she suggested to my mind. She looked embarrassed – got up restlessly – moved to the door. But she was too late. I'd got it. She looked exactly like someone who has just been through some awful experience of pain telling the next victim that it's his turn... Relieved for herself but knowing what she was sending me to... I was tremendously interested, too much so to speak.

At the door she turned.

"Shall I say you'll come?" she whispered.

"Oh, rather, please. May I send a note too? I mean – it's so awfully kind of your guardian to invite me. I'd like to thank her."

"Oh, I'll tell her," breathed Adela anxiously. "You needn't bother. I'll tell her. She'll be very pleased," she added; and at the words she did look a little easier.

When she was gone, I began to put things together. It came, I thought, to this – the kid must have been brought up in the firmest

150

manner by a Tartar of a guardian of whom she was, even now, mortally scared. She had probably never been allowed to have a friend, or even a possession, of her own. Then, when she was grown up, the dragon had seen her mistake, and had sent her to Oxford with the idea of developing her. She was probably pathetically anxious to see Adela launching out, making friends, being a success, when, owing to the training she had given her, the poor kid was completely incapable of doing anything of the kind. And Adela was still so terrified of this tyrant of her childhood that she had dreaded my refusing – dreaded having to confess that she had, so far, failed to take advantage of her opportunities. That accounted, too, for her odd look at me. Dreading her guardian as she clearly did, she disliked having to hand me over to her. The Subconscious, no doubt, I thought rather grandly. Subconsciously she associated her guardian with whippings, supperless bedtimes and scoldings, and still feared, both for herself and for me, the iron discipline of her childhood. I felt very much pleased with this reconstruction, it fitted all the facts (so far as I knew them) so admirably. I was sure I was right!

I felt quite unwarrantably excited as I arranged my journey to the Bedfordshire village where, it seemed, Adela and her guardian lived. I'd already told Maude Evans where I was going, and rejoiced to see her scepticism change to disappointment and a kind of sulky admiration. If I could get the invitation, I was sure, I thought, to get the confidences in the end; and clearly Maude thought so too. She was obviously very much annoyed – though she could quite well spare the fiver. This added to my pleasurable excitement, which had been considerable in any case, for I was really interested, and very keen to find out what Adela's background really was. I was sure my guess was right in the main, and I also felt that I might, with luck, be able to do something to set things right for the poor kid. I hate to see people as crushed as that, and I had, then, almost unlimited faith in my powers to please and cajole people, especially oldish ladies. I had, then, not the smallest doubt that I should be able to soothe and tame this particular dragon and make life much easier for her aggravatingly timid charge.

On the way down, and especially during the inevitable and interminable wait at Bletchley, I tried to extract something more from Adela about her home conditions. I particularly wanted to know whether there were any other members of the household; my campaign would rather depend on that. But Adela seemed terrified afresh by the very tactful questions I asked. "No – no one else – now... We... there were more of us – at one time..." And here her voice quite gave out, and her pale eyes filled with horror, gazing past me in blank misery.

Again I guessed – some appalling family tragedy, of which she was the sole survivor. Experience, memory, or a "complex" due to an ancient terror – that accounted for a lot. And, on top of it, this probably severe guardian... I was getting on. Soon, I felt, I should know enough to extract confidences! I was almost sorry when the train struggled in.

It was pretty full – there had been some local market somewhere – and it was quite impossible to talk. But I watched, surreptitiously, and I saw the pale, vague face opposite me grow paler and the eyes more strained and blank with every stage of our slow, jolting progress.

We were met at our station by an odd old cumbrous carriage, "handsome" to look at, but most depressing. One felt that it was quite inevitably connected with highly respectable funerals; you could almost smell black kid gloves and expensive wreaths. And our dead silence, broken only by Adela's hoarse, uneven breathing and the splash as we rumbled through puddles, only made it worse. I've seldom felt so uneasy – not alarmed, nothing so definite, but just indefinably uncomfortable, with a rather quickened heartbeat as we moved, ponderously and silently, along deserted lanes, wet with the cold rains of March, and between hedges dripping with evening mist.

The house was as large, solid, respectable, and nearly as depressing as the carriage. As we got out, Adela startled me by a sudden, feverish clutch at my hand; hers was dead cold. But before I could respond, the huge front door had swung silently open, and we were inside the house.

It was quite different inside – warm, almost to oppression, well-lighted, roomy. I hardly had time to notice more than this before I saw my hostess.

One generally, though often unconsciously, makes pictures in one's mind of what a stranger will look like. I hadn't known that I had made such a guess about Adela Young's guardian (whose very name I had not yet heard); I think perhaps I had a sort of Lady Dedlock, or even a Mrs. Reid, in my mind; but, as we entered the hall, comfortingly warm and bright after the misty fields and lanes, and I had my first glimpse of her, I knew at a glance that whatever I guessed had been wrong, for I could never, never have pictured such a person as I saw.

She remained sitting by the fire – a tiny, tiny little old lady, wrapped in a marvellous Eastern shawl; and the first thing that I thought was that she was tremendously, incredibly old – not "old" as one generally uses the word of people, but "old" as the pyramids and Stonehenge are old – timeless, ageless, and vital. And she was also – not beautiful – fascinating is the only word I can think of to express her face – a face "from which I could hardly take my eyes, it was at once so vivid and so inscrutable. When my first impressions settled into something more nearly approaching coherence, I thought I saw why that was. Her porcelain face was flushed, her tiny mouth scarlet, constantly moving, her motions all quick, precise, alert; but over her eyes she wore dark, blank glasses that gave her a secret look, rather dreadful.

As we came in, she moved round in her chair with one of the darting movements, between the movement of a bird and a snake, that, though they were startling at first, I soon got used to, they were so characteristic.

"Is that you, Adela? Have you brought Miss Yorke?"

Her voice was shallow, sweet and tremendously eager, but at the same time – what shall I say? – bodiless. From its eagerness I might have been a celebrity. Poor old thing, I thought, what a life she must lead when the visit of an Irish undergraduate thrills her like that!

"Yes," whispered Adela, hardly audibly. Her voice was so faint, so quavering, that I looked round at her sharply. Her face was ashen, her lips colourless, her eyes vacant as if with sheer naked panic. Her tongue passed incessantly over her white lips. She reminded me of a hypnotised rabbit.

"How very kind of her," murmured the old lady. "Bring her here, Adela – I can't come to you, Miss Yorke, you must forgive me – I'm an old woman – lame and blind..."

And sick, too, I thought, as I took her tiny shrunken hand, for it was burning as if with fever, and tremulous with something that I did not think was age alone. It was more like the quivering of intense excitement. What a life, I thought! What a life they must lead, those two women in that big, lonely comfortable house, when the young one was a mass of terrors and alarms and the old one feverish with excitement over a visit from a girl she could not even see!

"I can't see you with my eyes," the old lady said then. "I wonder if you will let me see you with my fingers? Will you let me feel your face?"

"Of course," I said, and knelt down beside her.

If I had guessed at all what that ordeal would be like, I would never have assented. I cannot describe the utter loathing and repulsion that filled me as the tiny, soft, hot hands passed like feathers over my face. It was horrible, sickening – like allowing some dreadful unclean insect to crawl about one's face, up to the roots of my hair, down my cheeks, round my eyes, along my chin and neck... I could hardly restrain my utter disgust, although, when at last her hands dropped, and I rose, rather unsteadily, to my feet, I could not understand my own loathing. I shook myself impatiently, angry at my own folly.

Fortunately, I didn't have to remain beside her for very long. She kept Adela – her gesture was at once commanding and excited, as she asked her to stop for a few minutes, though her voice was as soft and sweet as ever – and I was given over into the charge of an elderly, most respectable-looking maid; but she, too, was odd. She was quiet, efficient, everything she should have been: but she had the face of a sleepwalker. There was not a flicker of expression on it. Her eyes were open, but wholly expressionless; they might have been made of glass, except that they were dull, like the eyes of a dead animal. Quiet, orderly, deft as she was, she made me shiver a little. It was like being waited on by an automaton, or a somnambulist. I got rid of her as soon as I could, saying that I preferred to dress myself; and turning at once to the dressing-table; and it was then that I got a real shock. For, looking in the mirror, my back to her, I saw that she turned at the door, and I caught a glance of a white face distorted by a look of such malignance as I had never dreamed possible. It was utterly inhuman, devilish. I whipped round – but she had gone, the door closed silently behind her. I must have imagined it, I thought, taking up my brushes; some trick of reflection – some odd effect of the mingled twilight and electric light... I dressed quickly, though, and went downstairs as soon as I could. I felt I wanted company.

I remember practically nothing of that dinner, except the vivid, fascinating face of the old lady, surmounted by the terrible dark glasses. I don't remember even what we talked of; though I have a dim impression that the old lady did most of the talking and that her talk was extremely good. Adela, I think, said not one word. I remember nothing at all of her presence, except one glance, when, her guardian having turned aside to speak to a servant, I caught her eyes across the table and was shocked by the sheer despair of their terror. *Why?* What on earth was the matter with her? I felt impatient, almost angry; but the next moment I had forgotten her very existence in the charm (I use the word in its old sense) of the old lady's presence.

After I went to bed that night I could not sleep for thinking about this odd household. I lay for hours, it seemed to me, turning it over in my mind – that enchanting old lady, with the vivid face and blank eyes, the touch of her soft, wandering fingers on my face, the wonderful talk in the shallow, sweet, meaningless voice; Adela, scared, quivering and drab; the secretive, passive maid with that one malignant glance...

It had been a chilly month, but my room felt curiously close and warm. At home in Ireland, I always sleep out of doors, and, when I can, I get my bed out on a balcony even at college. I missed the cool freedom, I thought; so I got up to see if there were, by any chance, a balcony or even a ledge where I could sit for a bit.

There was – a narrow one, but wide enough to stand on. I got out of my window and stood there, enjoying the coolness. There must be central heating in the house, I thought, to get that oppressive heat... And then I heard voices.

"...Midsummer. You must bring her, do you hear?"

"Oh, I can't! I *can't*..."

That, I knew, was Adela, though I had never before heard her voice so loud or so urgent. It was almost a wail.

"Be quiet, you fool! It's either that, or you..."

I stepped over my sill again. I couldn't stand and listen. But I was more wide awake than ever. The other voice, though it had been only a whisper, was, I felt sure, the old lady's. There had been in it something chill, menacing, that made me feel cold even now.

What could it all be about? I, no doubt, was the person who was to be "brought" at Midsummer. But *why*? And why had Adela broken through her scared neutrality to cry, in that anguished wail, "*I can't?*" And what would happen if she didn't?

What was the choice suggested by that "It's either that, or you..."?

I am, I admit, curious by nature, and now I was thrilled, consumed by curiosity. My repulsion was gone in the sheer love of a mystery. For I felt sure that there was a real mystery here – it was not my imagination, but something real, actual, in this house – a mystery that concerned me, as well as Adela and the old lady. I *must* find out what it was. Adela was so docile, so entirely without the power of resistance; surely I could get it out of her? Surely I had a right to try, when it concerned myself? I determined, anyhow, that I would. Dawn had come when I fell asleep with that resolution.

Breakfast was brought to me in bed. I gathered, from the matter-of-fact way in which this was done, that it must be the rule of the house. I wasn't sorry; I was tired after my wakeful night, and besides I wanted to think things over, sort out my impressions, and, if it seemed necessary, get some sort of idea of what my plans should be. When I finally came down to the hall, I found the old lady in sole possession, established in her chair as she had been when we arrived. She might never have moved. I greeted her as cheerily as I could, and she called me over to her chair.

"Miss Yorke," she said, "I'm so glad to have you alone. I want to ask you something. You must forgive my springing things on you, but I don't want Adela to hear and I might not have another opportunity."

I murmured vaguely.

"Tell me," said the old lady – and her voice was urgent – "has Adela ever said anything to make you think that she might marry?"

"Why no!" I cried, astonished. *Adela* marry! You might as well suspect a faded lettuce of falling in love.

"Never? Not a hint?"

"Never. But we aren't at all – intimate, you know," I said. "She's never spoken at all of – of her personal affairs, her family or anything like that."

"No? No, perhaps she wouldn't. She's very shy," said the old lady, "and she had – a shock."

Her voice was quite ordinary, sweet, compassionate a little; but for an instant her lips were parted in a tiny smile, furtive, malicious and cold, and her little scarlet tongue flickered over her lips. "Listen, Miss Yorke," she went on, very earnestly. "I'm anxious about Adela. She has no relations – no one but me. I can't explain now, there isn't time. But, you see, I'm very old. I want Adela to marry – to marry *soon*," she added, and I could see her little wrinkled hands clutched on her stick.

"And is there anyone...?" I hesitated.

"Yes. There is. And I want it settled – at once."

Her voice was tense with her urgency.

"I want to lay my hands on her children," she added, in an extraordinary voice – "gloating" was the word that occurred to me. It ought to have been pathetic, her anxiety to feel, since she could not see, the children of the girl she had brought up; but it wasn't. It was sickening – nauseating. Why, I don't know – something in her voice or tone, or the greedy way in which her tiny aged hands tightened till the knuckles stood out like white pebbles.

"She's never said a word to me," I said, stupidly and coldly.

"No? Well, perhaps she will. If she does, Miss Yorke, urge her – urge her. Tell her she must, for her own sake."

It was the same voice I had heard last night – silky, cold and menacing. The voice that had said "It's either that, or you..."

I said nothing. There seemed to be nothing to say. And in the stubborn silence I felt – enmity. It seemed to last for minutes. Then,

"Thank you," said the sweet, shallow voice. "Thank you very much, Miss Yorke. I am counting on you."

She smiled again, and again her smile sickened me, it was so triumphant and so ruthless. Or so it seemed at the time. A few seconds later, when, with a muttered excuse about looking for Adela, I had escaped into the damp garden, I thought I was a fool – over-tired, probably, with term – ready to read mysteries into the most ordinary things. For after all, what was more natural than that the old lady should wish to see Adela's future safe before she died? – to touch, since she could not see, her children? What was there malignant in that? On the contrary, it was benevolent, rather pathetic. I felt very penitent over my own moodiness and (I feared) rudeness.

In fact, the more I thought of it, the more I saw how right the old lady was. Clearly, Adela's future would be pretty hopeless when her guardian was gone. Shyness, with her, was almost a mania. She would simply retire into herself, shut herself up here in the Bedfordshire house with the odd maid – go off her head, as likely as not. Myself, I should have thought marriage was an impossible idea for her; I could not imagine any man... But apparently there was one. She might be an heiress, you never knew. Not a very good motive for anyone to want to marry her, perhaps; but even so a marriage that was at all reasonably happy would be better than solitude and craziness. Why on earth had I so loathed the idea when the old lady mentioned it? Why had I been so utterly repelled by her? I could not imagine. What a fool I had been!

I wandered about the neglected garden, vaguely, with no purpose. I was trying to sort things out in my mind, and I hardly noticed where I went. It was not a very big garden, but it seemed so because it had been allowed to run wild; the long, wet grass and overgrown borders and dripping evergreens gave a depressing effect of decay and neglect and age. There were tall hedges and clumps of laurestinus and box and elder that would have made it a fine place for hide-and-seek – only no one could imagine children laughing and romping there. It was dead, as gardens are when houses have long stood empty – dead, and yet somehow furtive. I disliked it more and more; but still I strayed there simply because I hated the house, and the blank-eyed, sweet-voiced old lady, even more. Things are never so bad out-of-doors, I thought; and I also thought that I could not imagine anyone ever feeling really terrified out-of-doors – for I now admitted, although unconsciously, that in the house I had felt, suddenly and inexplicably, real fear such as I had never in my life known before.

The very next moment, I knew that I was wrong. Quite suddenly, without the least reason, I was cold and sick with sheer panic. It clutched my heart so that I could not breathe; sweat started out on my forehead and lips and arms. I heard my breath rasping in my throat, and the heavy, irregular thudding of my heart...

I stared round me wildly. If only I could *see* something, no matter how appalling – it would not be so bad. It was this terror of *nothing* that was so dreadful.

But there was nothing. Nothing. Long rank grass, hedged in by dark, dripping evergreens; a stone seat, low and broad and flat, the charred ring left by a weed fire, black in the long, rain-grey grass. Nothing else. Not a sound but the melancholy drip of the leaves – nothing. I stood there as if bewitched – I could not move, I could not even cry out. I felt soaked in evil...

And then, as suddenly, the charm was snapped. I heard a sound – a hurried, furtive, stumbling step, a little whimpering sobbing noise – and I could move again. I turned and ran, gasping and shaking, out of the silent, evil enclosure – and ran straight into Adela.

She shrieked – such a shriek as I never wish to hear again – and immediately clapped both her hands to her mouth, crushing back the sound. Her eyes stared, terrified, over her hands.

I caught at her as if she were my salvation.

"Adela," I gasped – I could not speak – "Adela – what is it – in there – in this house? *What is it?*"

She stared dumbly back. I shook her arm, dragging her hands down from her shaking lips.

"Tell me," I urged. "Who is she? What is it?"

"Oh, Honor, don't – I don't know – what do you mean? Oh, don't ask me – don't – I don't know..."

"You do know. What is it? What is going to happen at Midsummer?"

She still stared back, horror in her eyes, her white lips moving inaudibly.

"What do you know?" she whispered at last. I could only just hear the words.

"I know there's devilry going on in this house," I said, "and I know that I'm in it... Look here, Adela; we must work together. You must help me. We can stop it – we will. Only we'll have to be quick. Tell me. Who is she? What is it?"

She still stared back, too scared to speak.

I don't know what put the words into my head.

"It isn't only me," I said, "it's you, Adela – and your children."

She gasped at that, and her cold hands clutched at me.

"I know, I know!" she babbled in a whisper I could hardly hear. "She will, I know... Honor, what can we do? She's listening even now. She can hear and see everything we do... We can't ever get away from her. She – she wants another, Honor. It's the year – it's five years since... Listen. She got us when we were babies, my brothers and me. I don't know why. I was only three. Two years, later..."

She broke off, gulping.

I shook her arm again.

"Go on," I said.

She glanced at me, and then away, her eyes staring before her.

"He died – Phil, the youngest. He – they said he fell – on the shears – there, in the enclosure there. His throat – they said it was pierced. I think I knew even then – I was a baby, but I think I knew – it wasn't as they said... I knew things, even then. Afterwards..."

Again she broke off, shaking all over.

"Five years after that," she went on – and again she stopped.

"Yes? Yes?" I urged her.

"It was Leslie next," she whispered. "It – an operation, she said – her own doctor – it satisfied people... But I knew, Honor, I *knew* – and he did, I think... And then, five years ago, Stephen... the one just older than me... They said it was suicide... Honor, oh, Honor, it wasn't, it *wasn't*. She..."

She sobbed, one deep, heavy sob.

"It was there – where you came from just now – oh, you frightened me so – I thought it was... It was there, Honor, one Midsummer night. I saw smoke. I guessed. I knew it was Stephen – the five years were over. I knew it was danger – oh, horrible, you don't know. I knew a good deal then... I was in bed, but I ran and ran... Stephen – I thought – I ran, hoping all the time... My feet were all cut next day..."

Her voice died away in a little sobbing whisper.

"It was – over... I saw her – and the fire – and the stone bench... Oh, Honor!"

She clutched at me again, staring as if she still saw that horror.

"She knew I was there," she went on at last. I could hardly hear her shaken whisper. "She never hid anything after that. I've seen – everything... And now – she – the next five years are up."

I felt cold and very sick.

"It's to be me," I whispered.

Adela nodded.

"That's why I was sent," she said at last, "to get someone. I tried not to, Honor, I did try. I couldn't help it. I had to do it... You see – she wants to keep me – she wants children – little children – ready..."

We stared at each other in hopeless horror.

"She knows everything I do and say and think," Adela went on in the same hurried gabbling whisper. "She knows we're here now, talking of it. She knows everything, Honor. We can't ever – oh what can I do? What can I do?"

Her despair roused me.

"We have till Midsummer," I said. "We'll be ready by then."

But she shook her head hopelessly.

"You don't know," she said. "You don't understand. She sees your thoughts. You can't plan against her."

"We can," I asserted, "and we will."

She looked up, a glimmer of hope in her questioning eyes.

"It'll be all right," I said. "I'll get you out of it."

And linking my arm in hers I led her back to the house.

I can't find words to say how I dreaded entering it, facing the old lady who, according to Adela, knew all we had done and said. But Adela's presence made it easier. Anyhow I knew what I was up against, and I knew that someone weaker than I depended on me. You can't have better incentives to courage. So when we met the old lady face to face in the porch I was able to open my attack right away. I was astonished to hear how natural my voice was as I spoke.

"I did meet Adela, you see," I said, "and we've been having a lovely long talk. She's been awfully kind – she says she'd like me to come again. I wonder if I really may?"

"I should be delighted if you would," purred the old lady, with her polite, surface smile. I wondered with one part of my mind if she really could see into my mind and read my thoughts. "When can you manage it?"

"We go down on the twentieth of June," I said. "Could I come straight to you then on the twentieth?"

I heard Adela give a terrified gasp, and her hand, tucked under my elbow, clutched my arm convulsively. The old lady's blank, black glasses above her shallow smile made me shiver a little; I had the impression that, owing to their very emptiness, they read me and concealed their knowledge. But I kept a hold on myself, thanks to Adela's trembling hand in my arm; I think there was not even a tremor in my voice as I made all the arrangements and polite speeches that one does make when one fixes up a visit.

We went back to Oxford that afternoon, and after that, I returned to Connemara for the rest of the vac. And, during those few weeks, I thought it all out. Finally I took my twin brother Conal into my secret. I knew he would know that I hadn't panicked over nothing and that he would help me to pull through. We spent long afternoons in the glens with a wise man. My family chaffed me about my sudden interest in fairy lore. I left Conal to carry on our preparations and went back to Oxford for the Summer Term.

One's first summer term generally seems to stand out in people's memory. Mine is a blank. I could think of nothing but what was to come on the day after term ended on Midsummer Day. And I was not helped to forget it by Adela, who followed me round with mute, imploring, adoring eyes and half-begun, quavering sentences that she never completed. I nearly lost my patience with her more than once, and begged her not to destroy the little nerve I had left. After all it was my risk, not hers, and I'd seen – and, even worse, felt – quite enough to make it unnecessary and maddening to hear her constant appeals – "Oh, Honor, do take care – oh, don't try it – you don't understand..." I was determined to take every possible care, but I was equally determined to see the business through.

I don't believe Adela and I exchanged a single word on our journey down to Bedfordshire on that twentieth of June. It was a steamy, breathless day – not a leaf stirring on the heavy trees, the streams crawling sluggishly between the fields where the very grass was motionless. I hoped for thunder vaguely; and with all my might I hoped and prayed that Conal had managed his part of the business. I had said nothing about him, or our plans, to Adela, because I now believed that, owing to her long subjection and terror, her mind was really open to her terrible guardian even when they were apart. But my mind was free, my own; I was strong and independent; so I made my plans – and kept them entirely to myself. All I had said to Adela was that she was to slip out of the house at midnight and remain away from it. I had learnt that all the servants left it each evening – I could guess why.

The house seemed asleep, in a heavy, enchanted torpor that was, as it were, embodied in the thick flowery patens and sickly, pungent scent of the elder trees about it. It was silent, motionless. In the airless heat I felt my hands and feet dead cold. It was sinister – evil. It had not been like that before, I thought stupidly; it was as if the heat drew out some evil emanation as it drew the scent from the elder blossoms. My feet seemed turned to lead, heavy, cold. I could hardly drag them along. I felt drugged, stupefied, by the scent that enveloped the house and by the heat that only seemed to touch the outside of me and left an icy core of fear within. I kept thinking, all that dreadful evening, "Five hours more – only four hours now..." as the time loitered by and midnight approached.

I don't remember much of the evening except that I heard my own voice making conversation, and remember being vaguely surprised to hear how easy and ordinary it sounded. I remember wondering if I had developed a dual personality. My mind felt like my body – giving normal reactions on the surface, while deep down in the centre it was frozen by sheer unnameable terror. I still dream sometimes of that hot, airless evening, with the smell of the elders outside the windows, and the smooth flow of mechanical talk concealing hatred and horror under a mask as smooth and thin as silk.

The sky darkened slowly, and at ten, I made my excuses. I said I was tired – the weather made me headachey – might I go to bed? I smothered a yawn convincingly. The old lady was very solicitous, and, I thought, relieved. I was urged to go to bed at once – she would send me hot milk and a mild sleeping draught. I thanked her, accepted everything, and went to my room.

I wondered, as I undressed, whether I should take that sleeping draught. Suppose Conal failed... I felt so sick at the thought that I had to sit down – I was trembling too much to stand. I felt despairing now. The house had sucked away my courage and my hope. I knew, now, that I was doomed as those others had been doomed... We would fail – we must. What could we do against – *that?* I would be sacrificed as Adela's brothers had been – as her children would be. Would I not be better drugged, only half aware of the final horror?

I stood hesitating, the draught in my hand. All my pluck was gone... I can't describe the awful abyss of sheer terror that engulfed me. I heard myself whimpering a little, like a terrified dog, and felt my face twitching. I couldn't, *couldn't* do it – that terrible little enclosure, hedged by the secret shrubs – the fire – the stone bench

– I couldn't – I couldn't...

Then the idea of Conal came into my mind. I mustn't let him down. I had my part to play. If I were a heavy, unconscious lump I might fail him just when he needed me. That braced me at once. I could do it now. I knew how I would have looked and felt if I had yielded to the temptation and taken the drug – I had seen myself as clearly as if I had stood beside my own drugged body. I could do it, and I would. I should not fail... I undressed and lay down in the bed. Somewhere in the silent house a clock tolled half past ten. My agony had lasted only a few minutes, and – I had to wait till midnight. I can't attempt to describe those crawling minutes – the alternation of determination and overwhelming terror, of the picture of the secret, evil enclosure, and of my brother. At last I heard the heavy, boding stroke – a quarter to twelve. My time had come. Any minute now...

A step in the passage – light, shuffling, furtive. I relaxed every muscle; I half buried my face in the pillow, breathing slowly and heavily, and rejoicing that I had thought of smearing the edges of my lips with the pungent drug she had given me. The door opened inch by inch. I wondered if she could hear my heart thumping in the dead silence.

Not a sound. Had she gone? If only I dared look! It was awful, wondering and waiting. Had she gone? Or was she there, beside me, watching me..? No sound. I had to keep relaxing my muscles; they stiffened as soon as I listened. And I had to go on breathing steadily, quietly...

I nearly screamed when I felt a cold, light touch on my neck. I was just able to turn it into a restless sign and the little movement of a heavy sleeper settling again to slumber.

"Take the head," came a bodiless whisper. "We have only just time."

Hands were slipped under my shoulders; other hands – tiny, cold, soft hands – took my feet. I could hardly bear that cold, soft ruthless touch. I knew whose hands they were...

They carried me downstairs. I think they were too heavily burdened – or perhaps too anxious – to notice how, twice, I forgot and found my muscles tense with loathing and terror. I lay, for most of that awful journey, limp and relaxed, breathing as if asleep, with my heart in my throat with terror.

We were out of doors. There was no stir of air, but it felt different, and the scent of the elders was heavier, more cloying than ever. On and on, through the rank grass that smelt of dew as they pressed it; over a path that gave a dull echo to their shuffling feet; through a gap in a hedge that smelt stuffily of evergreens...

They laid me on the stone bench. I could feel it, cold and rough, through my thin nightgown; and then – can hardly bear to remember it – I smelt thick, heavy smoke and heard the rasp of steel on stone...

I could not endure another instant. I leapt up and shrieked – shrieked the words I had learned – heard a crash...

I don't remember anything more. All I know is that Conal had not failed me. He, outside that evil enclosure, had done his part as I had done mine within. It was over... An hour later the house was roaring in flame to the darkened sky, while lightning flickered overhead and Adela crouched weeping beside me...

I was ill after that, and went up late next term. Almost the first person I met was Maude Evans.

"Hullo!" she said. "Better?"

I said I was all right.

"Fancy you being so upset about a fire!" she said. "But there was a death in it, wasn't there?" she added, as an extenuation.

"Yes," I said.

"You were there when it broke out, weren't you?" she went on.

"Oh yes. I was staying there. You've lost your fiver all right," I said, hoping that would make her sheer off. But it didn't. She had clearly forgotten the fiver, and was rather crestfallen, but looking for a loophole at once.

"Well, but did the Young kid ever confide anything to you?" she demanded. "That was part of it, you know."

I shivered a little.

"Oh yes, she confided in me all right," I said.

"Really intimate?"

"Oh yes – very. Too intimate to tell you, Maude."

Maude scowled sulkily.

"Men?" she asked then.

Again I shivered.

"Well," I said, "marriage came into it."

RANDALLS ROUND
AFTERWORD

Eleanor Scott followed the splendid literary tradition of the great Victorian women authors, notably Elizabeth Gaskell, Mary E. Braddon, Amelia B. Edwards, Charlotte Riddell and Margaret Oliphant, who all created some of the finest ghost stories ever written.

She was one of the best, but ultimately least known, writers in this genre during the 1920s. With the fleeting appearance of her only collection – *Randalls Round* – she was never as prolific as her great contemporaries, E. F. Benson, H. Russell Wakefield, A. M. Burrage, Marjorie Bowen, Margery Lawrence, L. P. Hartley, and the most important and admired of all – M. R. James.

His influence is clearly evident in several of Eleanor Scott's stories. The Biblical and antiquarian research leading to the climactic emergence of the hideous slimy creature from a deep hole in the wall in 'The Twelve Apostles' can be seen as an ingenious pastiche of 'The Treasure of Abbot Thomas'. Jamesian buffs will also spot similarities between MRJ's Parkins and Maddox in '*Celui-là*' ('That One'), and the small Breton village of Kerouac is not unlike Burnstow in 'Oh, Whistle, and I'll Come to You, My Lad' with its long unfrequented beach; but Scott always adds several new and disturbing touches, inspired by her own constant bad dreams.

'Eleanor Scott' was the pseudonym of Helen M. Leys, born on 11 July 1892 at the family home, Richmond Villa in Hampton Hill, Middlesex. Although her middle name was registered as 'Madeline', she always used the alternative 'Magdalen' when signing official documents throughout her adult life. She had three brothers (and two elder step-brothers) and was particularly close to her only sister, Mary Dorothy Rose Leys, who later became a highly regarded historian.

Their father John Kirkwood Leys (1847-1909) was a former barrister who became a popular novelist, beginning with *The Lindsays: a romance of Scottish Life* (1888; 3 volumes), and then moving on to a long run of exciting thrillers including *The Lawyer's Secret* (1897), *The Black Terror: a romance of Russia* (1899), *The House-Boat Mystery* (1905) and *The Missing Bridegroom* (1908). Both his daughters had active and lively imaginations, and it is known that Mary invented and provided several plots for these Edwardian thrillers, and it is quite likely that Helen (two years younger than Mary) also helped her father with plot-lines, especially for his last adventure story – written specifically for children – *By Creek and Jungle* (1909).

After the sudden death of John Kirkwood Leys, his widow Ellen was forced to follow his example by writing stories and novelettes which helped to keep ahead of the weekly bills. In a private unpublished memoir Helen's brother Duncan Leys recalled that their remarkable and hard-working mother "almost unaided prepared my sisters for their university scholarship examinations. Neither of them ever went to school; she taught them Latin, French, English language and literature, elementary mathematics, geography, music, and, of course, earlier on, reading and writing... The sisters were clever and original, and both of them became scholars at Oxford colleges (Somerville and St. Hilda's)".

Both Mary and Helen developed a keen interest in history and geography, and Helen was especially devoted to the subject of women travellers and explorers (which eventually led to two books on these themes). In spite of winning an Oxford scholarship, Helen later joked (to her niece Susan) with undue modesty that "the only prize she ever won was for milking a cow"! This probably suggests that she worked as a landgirl on a farm during the First World War. Her elder brother Colin was killed in action on the Somme in 1916, while her youngest brother Alan was severely wounded but managed to survive.

After the war Helen became a full-time teacher, and this eventually blossomed into her main career (from the 1930s onwards) as a Vice-Principal, and later Principal, of a teacher training college in Oxfordshire.

Her first ghost story to appear in print was 'The Room', a well-constructed example of the standard "haunted room" sub-genre which had reached its apex in Lanoe Falconer's classic *Cecilia de Noel* (1891). Credited to H. M. Leys, 'The Room' made its debut in the prestigious *Cornhill Magazine* in October 1923.

Although H. M. Leys never reappeared in the pages of the *Cornhill*, 'The Room' was obviously much liked by the publishers and readers alike, as it was soon reprinted by the anonymous editor Leonard Huxley in his anthology *Sheaves from the Cornhill* (John Murray, 1926; reissued 1928).

The career of 'Eleanor Scott' as a mainstream novelist covered barely seven years, beginning with the controversial *War Among Ladies*, published by Ernest Benn in 1928. This is an extremely heartfelt and angry work on school life, written with great feeling by one who was obviously very familiar – on a daily basis – with the subject matter. The story's heroine, the unfortunate Miss Cullen, may be strongly autobiographical. As a professional teacher, Helen Leys naturally had to disguise her true identity completely under a *nom de plume*, and the link between the two names was never revealed publicly in her lifetime.

The anonymous reviewer in the *Times Literary Supplement* declared that "*War Among Ladies* is not so much a novel as a piece of propaganda. Miss Eleanor Scott's chief purpose is to move our indignation against the evils of the High School system. She uses her imagination as a weapon of offence, and not for its own sake... She makes us live for a time in Besley High School and understand as if from our own experience the half-insane hostilities which are possible in such a place. Miss Scott describes this peculiar atmosphere at least as vividly as Mr Hugh Walpole in *Mr Perrin and Mr Traill*."

The novel received several other good reviews including V. Sackville-West's observation that "Miss Eleanor Scott is a very able writer"; and these probably encouraged Ernest Benn to publish *Randalls Round* in the following year. 'The Room' from the *Cornhill* was here joined by eight previously unpublished stories and a short foreword which memorably described the origins of these tales in her terrifying dreams.

When *Randalls Round* was published in September 1929 it was not marketed as a horror collection, and the phrase "ghost stories" appeared nowhere. The jacket picture portraying the title story (with dancing villagers around the pole surmounted by an ox's head and shaggy hide, the man in bull's head standing behind the mysterious white-shrouded figure) conveyed no terror at all, almost giving the appearance of a bucolic children's book.

No reviewers of the time seemed to appreciate that these stories, especially 'The Twelve Apostles', 'At Simmel Acres Farm', and '*Celui-là*' (rather than being a mere pastiche of 'Oh, Whistle, and I'll Come to You, My Lad') were superlative uncanny tales and ghost stories in their own right; but the *Times Literary Supplement* asserted that the author's disturbing dreams in one or two cases had a traceable literary origin – "for instance, 'The Old Lady' puts one in mind of a story by Walter de la Mare" ('Seaton's Aunt'), "and her giant slugs and wicked Latin manuscripts are not without parallel"!

Honor Yorke in 'The Old Lady' and Annis Breck in '"Will Ye No' Come Back Again?"' are both emancipated young Oxford women clearly based on the author herself, while *sacrificium hominum* is a recurring theme in the majority of these tales, especially in 'The Cure', 'At Simmel Acres Farm', '*Celui-là*', and the title story.

If Eleanor Scott's stories do not fully convey the horrors of her nightmares, as she suggests in her pithy foreword, those nightmares must have been terrifying indeed! Perhaps the publication of the nine tales in *Randalls Round* helped to exorcise the horrors in her dreams, as apparently she wrote no more stories of this kind after 1929.

A. D. Marks, the managing director of Ernest Benn at the time of *Randalls Round's* publication, became a director of Philip Allan & Co. Ltd. in 1930. This company published the bestselling series of 'Creeps' anthologies from 1932 to 1936, and it is tempting to surmise that Marks may well have encouraged Eleanor Scott to contribute several new supernatural horror stories under different pseudonyms. Some of the 'Creeps' tales, especially those by the unknown N. Dennett, are very similar in style to those in *Randalls Round*; but this conjecture is impossible to prove now after seventy-five years.

Eleanor Scott's second novel, *The Forgotten Image*, was published by Benn in April 1930. The title alludes to the image described by St James as the "natural face" which a person sees in the mirror and at once forgets. The story is set in an East End settlement, Frobisher House, and details the vocation of Alison Chambers for social work and her friendship with Beryl Chambers, who in turn has a deep infatuation for an older woman, Pauline Frobisher.

This book made little impression and, like its two predecessors, was quickly remaindered. Following the departure of A. D. Marks, Benn was no longer interested in any more fiction by Eleanor Scott, and there was a hiatus of nearly three years before Helen could find another publisher, Hamish Hamilton, who issued her last three novels in quick succession: *Swings and Roundabouts* (March 1933), *Beggars Would Ride* (October 1933) and *Puss in the Corner* (November 1934).

Puss in the Corner was an insightful study of a widowed mother and her two unmarried daughters. This mother, Ianthe Fraser, has always enjoyed the adoring affection of her husband, a well-known popular author. At his death she is left with two daughters in their late teens, Karen and Anna. Eventually Karen takes a position at the local school while Anna goes to teach at some distance away, but neither girl is happy. Anna is entangled in an unwelcome love-affair and longs for home. Karen finds the strain of teaching at school while keeping house for an untidy and selfish mother too much for her, and the girls change places. One can only speculate on how much of this story-line was autobiographical, or pure fiction.

Following the poor sales of her novels, Eleanor Scott found a much wider market with her two forays into non-fiction - the only real "bestsellers" in her brief writing career - *Adventurous Women* (1933) and *Heroic Women* (1939), Volumes 18 and 54 in the 'Nelsonian Library', both gift-books nicely produced by Thomas Nelson with colour plates. In 1937 she was awarded first prize in Nelson's competition for the best introduction – under her own name, H. M. Leys – to a volume in their series of literary classics. This essay, on Daniel Defoe's *A Journal of the Plague Year*, was also printed in *John o'London's Weekly* on 13 August 1937.

By the time Helen Leys had completed her last book, her elder sister Mary was achieving much acclaim for her academic historical studies. The books of M. D. R. Leys (as she was customarily known) include *Men, Money and Markets* (1936), *Between Two Empires: France, 1814-48* (1955), and *Catholics in England, 1559-1829: A Social History* (1961). She also wrote the definitive study on *A History of London Life* (1958) in collaboration with her sister-in-law Rosamund J. Mitchell (Mrs Alan Leys). Among R. J. Mitchell's best works are a biography of *John Tiptoft, Earl of Worcester* (1938), who was both William Caxton's patron and Britain's nearest equivalent to Vlad the Impaler during his reign of terror in Ireland; and *The Spring Voyage* (1964) on the Jerusalem Pilgrimage in 1458, in which Tiptoft also participated.

After the Second World War, the two sisters Mary and Helen lived together for several years in Oxford, and (following their retirement) then moved to Burton Lodge in Exmouth, Devon. Helen died at the Royal Devon & Exeter Hospital on 15 March 1965.

Eleanor Scott's tales of terror and the supernatural were unjustly neglected for many years until the 1970s when Hugh Lamb reprinted the finest examples in his excellent anthologies, beginning with *A Tide of Terror*. Both the 1929 first edition and the 1996

Canadian edition (Ash-Tree Press; limited to 500 copies) are now highly sought-after collectors items, fetching three figure sums.

In this new edition, the first to be published in Britain for over eighty years, *Randalls Round* should once again bring "an agreeable shudder or two" to new readers, and delight all connoisseurs of the early 20th-century ghost story.

Richard Dalby

Thank you for choosing this book – I hope you enjoyed it. Please be sure to visit oleanderpress.com to sign up for our infrequent, non-spammy Newsletter and get:

A free classic text
Updates on new, upcoming titles
Complete list of all horror titles
Pre-order discounts
Special Offers
Exclusive Offers

As well as news of other Oleander titles.

For further benefits:

facebook.com/oleanderpress
Twitter.com/oleanderman

I'd also appreciate any comments – good and bad – on the current list and welcome ideas for new classic titles to publish –

info@oleanderpress.com

I look forward to hearing from you!

Jon Gifford

Publisher,
Oleander Press

Made in the USA
Lexington, KY
04 January 2019